BEYOND PLATO'S CAVE

THE PHILOSOPHY CLUB - BOOK ONE

GRANT MAXWELL

PERSISTENT PRESS

est. 2012

ISBN: 1723220671

ISBN-13: 978-1723220678

Persistent Press
Nashville, Tennessee 37206
www.PersistentPress.com

TO MY SONS, MASON AND DYLAN

PART ONE

CHAPTER ONE
FIRST DAY

Ethan and Nick were up by a point with three seconds left on the clock. Nick served the ball, and their opponent smacked the glowing orb directly at their goal. Ethan dove, blocking the shot just in time. "Nice save!" Nick shouted as the buzzer went off. They had won the match! Then Ethan heard a distant voice.

"Time to go, honey!"

"See you at school, Nick!" Ethan called to his friend. He tore off his goggles and gloves, and shouted, "Coming, Mom!" as he grabbed his backpack and ran down the stairs two at a time.

It was Ethan Whitehead's first day of eighth grade. He was a little nervous to start a new school in a new city, but he was mostly excited to be reunited with his best friend, Nick Hillman. Ethan had left behind some pretty good friends in Boston, where he grew up, but he and Nick had known each other since they were babies, and they were two of a kind. Their dads had been roommates when they studied computer science at Stanford. Ethan's dad, David Whitehead, had become a professor at MIT after finishing his PhD. That's where he met Ethan's mom, Christina, another brilliant computer scientist. Nick's dad, Rob Hillman, had stayed in Silicon Valley and become a tech billionaire. He was the founder of The Scape, the most popular Virtual Reality system in the world. But the two geniuses had stayed close friends. Their families vacationed together every year on Nick's family's private island in the Caribbean.

Ethan's parents had invented an amazing new Virtual Reality interface called Mentalink. It was a huge leap beyond the goggles, headphones, and touchgloves that were the current standard. According to their dads, it was like being in another world. Ethan and Nick had spent a lot of time together in the Scapes, the virtual worlds created by Nick's dad. So even though their bodies had been across the country from each other, they had already been through a lot of adventures together. They felt as close as brothers. In fact, they were the closest thing each of them had to a brother, since neither of them had any real siblings.

Nick's dad had finally convinced Ethan's parents to move back to California to combine their new technology and Rob's software, games that were often more like worlds they could explore. And of course Rob Hillman's business skills and his huge fortune were a nice bonus. They were going to create a tech revolution. They all knew it.

The first day of classes went by in a blur. Ethan knew he was supposed to be overwhelmed starting a new school. But finally having Nick there by his side, cracking jokes and talking constantly about every possible thing made Ethan feel better than he had in a long time. Ethan, with his dark hair and olive skin, was quiet and shy. His prominent nose was often stuck in a book when he wasn't riding his bike or exploring the Scapes with Nick. Nick, with his dirty-blond hair and California tan, was outgoing. In Ethan's experience, Nick could talk anyone into anything and make them think it was their idea. They were a perfect match.

The last period of the day was Intro to Philosophy, and Nick led the way to the far side of the classroom to some open desks next to two girls. "Hey Izzy, hey Sophie," Nick called out breezily. "This is my best friend, Ethan. He just moved here from Boston."

"It's Isabella, actually, but everyone calls me Izzy," said the girl with curly brown hair and a wry smile, leaning forward. "Welcome to paradise." Ethan liked her right away. She reminded him of his cousin from New York.

"Hi," said Sophie in a calm voice, her long, dark red hair framing her pale, unreadable face. He noticed with a start that she was really pretty, like some medieval English princess. Ethan managed to get out a "hi," and then busied himself taking out the first book on the reading list, Plato's *Republic*.

"Alright, folks, I'm Mr. Gebser," said the teacher, who looked like a slightly graying surfer dude. "Today I'm going to tell you one of the most famous stories in the history of philosophy, Plato's Allegory of the Cave." Izzy rolled her eyes at Nick and mouthed the word "boring," but Nick just smiled. Ethan actually thought it sounded kind of interesting.

"There are people chained up in a cave, facing the wall with their backs to the cave's entrance. Outside the mouth of the cave, there's a huge bonfire, and people are carrying objects across the entrance so that they cast shadows on the wall. The people chained up have been there their whole lives, so they think the shadows are the real thing. Then one brave soul, a philosopher, gets the idea to break out of his chains and go check out what's going on outside the cave. He stumbles toward the opening, and at first he can't see a thing because he's blinded by the light. But as his eyes adjust, he sees people carrying these objects past that aren't just flat, grey shadows, but colorful three-dimensional objects. This is the World of Forms, which are more real than the shadows. And guess what?" Mr. Gebser paused for dramatic effect. "The word 'educate' comes from the Latin 'to lead out,' as in the philosopher who leads his buddies out of the cave into the real world."

Ethan thought that was pretty cool, and Sophie seemed to be listening closely, but Nick and Izzy were passing notes back and forth, quietly giggling. "And," Mr. Gebser continued, "that's what I'm trying to do with you jokers," he said, smiling benignly, looking directly at Izzy and Nick, who immediately fell silent. "I'm trying to lead you young scholars from the darkness into the light."

After the bell rang, Nick, never shy, asked the girls if they'd like to come over and play the new version of Glow Ball, one of his dad's most popular games.

Izzy, equally bold, said, "Sure! We love Glow Ball! You want to, Sophie?"

Sophie shrugged slightly and glanced over at Ethan with a reserved smile. "Yeah, OK."

CHAPTER TWO
THROUGH THE PARK

The four thirteen-year-olds unchained their bikes and walked them down the path around the back of the school, which led directly into the park, a few dozen acres of winding paths through redwood trees. Nick, as usual, kept up a steady stream of words, with Izzy throwing in frequent comments. "Izzy, Sophie, and I have known each other since preschool," Nick told Ethan, "but we haven't been hanging out that much the last few years. You know, boys against girls, that whole thing."

"Our parents work at Nick's dad's company," added Izzy. "My mom is the company's top lawyer, and Sophie's dad runs the design division."

"They design the Scapes," said Sophie. "My dad actually came up with the idea for Glow Ball based on a game the ancient Mayan people played in Central America." She seemed to light up talking about her dad's work.

"That's so cool!" Ethan said, and they grinned at each other for a moment before Nick continued with his tour-guide monologue.

"Here on your right are the Caves," Nick said, and pointed down a path into a slight ravine that led to an opening in the side of the hill. "There are a bunch of caverns in there that go for miles under the whole town."

"Have you ever gone in?" Ethan asked.

"Yeah, but only a little way," Nick replied. "I've heard it's like a maze in there."

"Cool."

Around the next bend in the path, they came to a playground where four high school kids were hanging out on the swings, smoking cigarettes: a thin, strikingly attractive blond boy and girl who looked like brother and sister, a big jock-looking guy with a buzz cut, and a gaunt, pale boy with long stringy black hair. They were all tall and wearing expensive-looking clothes, and they had a disdainful air about them.

"Hey, Tricky Nicky," sneered the handsome blond boy, "is that your little girlfriend?" gesturing with his chin toward Izzy as he took a drag off his cigarette.

"None of your business!" shouted Izzy fiercely.

"Nerd love," the pretty blond girl said with a condescending smile. "How sweet," and her friends laughed derisively as she looked the girls up and down, saving a special smile for Sophie, her eyes tight with amusement.

"Just leave us alone!" Nick snapped.

The blond boy's face abruptly changed from a lazy sneer to cruel anger, and he jumped up from the swing and threw down his cigarette. "Hey, Tricky Nicky, I want to ask you something." And he strode toward the younger boy who was standing over on the path.

"Come on, let's get out of here," Nick called to his friends, and they jumped on their bikes and sped away before the blond boy could reach them.

"Leaving so soon?" the blond boy shouted after them mockingly. "But we were just starting to have fun!"

Nick, Ethan, Sophie, and Izzy pedaled furiously along the path for a few minutes until they emerged from the trees onto a quiet street. They all stopped for a minute, panting, and Ethan asked, "What's up with those jerks?"

"Those are the Peterson twins, Connor and Abigail," explained Nick, "and their friends Milo Spencer, the one with long black hair who's always getting in trouble, and Stefan Rogan, who has more muscles than brains. They're ninth graders at our school. They're always trying to give me a hard time."

"Why do they hate you so much?" asked Ethan.

"The twins' dad, Jay Peterson, used to own the biggest Virtual Reality company in the Valley, at least before my dad decided to branch out from solar panels and self-driving cars to VR. The Scape system makes their dad's system look like *Pac Man*."

"What's *Pac Man*?" asked Sophie.

"It's an old arcade game from when our parents were kids," explained Izzy.

"Yeah, we have one in our Game Room," said Nick casually. "It's fun, but pretty basic. So anyway, Jay hates my dad. I guess he thinks he stole his thunder or something."

"But that doesn't make any sense!" said Sophie with a perplexed look. "Your dad can't help it if he invented a better system."

"I know," said Nick, "but I think he's holding a major grudge, and so the twins hate me too. Like father, like son and daughter, I guess."

"I guess," said Sophie, shaking her head. "That girl creeps me out. They kind of look like vampires," she mused. Izzy let out an awkwardly loud laugh reminiscent of a honk, but she did it with such confidence and joy that Ethan found himself copying it in a more subdued way. They all laughed good-naturedly, shaking off the experience with the bullies, and Sophie looked at Ethan with a steady, penetrating smile that made him blush slightly and look down.

"We're all going to be best friends," Izzy proclaimed with utter certainty, and though Nick threw a slightly skeptical smirk in her direction, they all knew it was true.

CHAPTER THREE
THE GAME ROOM

They walked their bikes a few blocks to Nick's house, a huge edifice of glass and steel that looked more like an art museum than a place to live, set back from the road surrounded by redwoods. When they went inside, their housekeeper, Blue, an Irish woman in her thirties with pink hair, was cutting vegetables in the big kitchen with the radio playing in the background. "Hey, Nicky! Hey, Ethan!" Blue called out in her Irish accent. "Who are your friends?"

Blue had been Nick's nanny when he was little, but they called her the housekeeper now that he was getting older, though she still kept an eye on him. Ever since he was a baby, but especially since Nick's parents had gotten divorced two years ago, Blue had been sort of like a second mother to Nick, or maybe a cool aunt, turning him on to older bands and making sure his style was always on point. Nick loved his mom, of course, but she was a movie actress, always off on location somewhere halfway around the world starring in some critically acclaimed blockbuster. The divorce had been really hard, but there hadn't been a lot of fighting, and it wasn't a big surprise. His dad was always working and his mom was always away, so it had just been him and Blue in the huge house a lot of the time, and him and Ethan in the Scapes.

Nick introduced Sophie and Izzy to Blue, who said, "Of course I remember you girls! You all used to play together when you were little. You've both grown up so much! Such beautiful young ladies," and she gave them all a warm smile. "Ethan, your parents are coming over for dinner. Let me know if I can make any of you a snack."

"OK, thanks, Blue!" Nick called out as they ran down the stairs to the basement. When they burst into the Game Room, Izzy exclaimed, "Woah! This is crazy!" Nick had never wanted for anything, but his parents had tried very hard not to spoil him. After the divorce, though, his dad had started having every imaginable game delivered to the house, enough to line the edges of the large, high-ceilinged room. Along one wall were about ten classic arcade games, from *Pac Man* and *Space Invaders* to *Joust* and *Tron*. Along another wall, there were bookshelves filled with paperbacks, magazines, and board games. Over in one corner, there was a ping-pong table and a foosball table, and in another corner was a big TV with what seemed like every game system ever invented arrayed around it on the floor, from Atari and the Nintendo Entertainment System to PlayStation 7 and Xbox Infinity. Above the TV was a giant framed black-and-white photo of the early

Beatles, with their mod suits and their moptop hair. "Nick and I are huge Beatles fans," Ethan explained.

To the side of the TV was a big wooden table with about eight sets of VR gear for going in the Scapes. "Let's play Glow Ball!" Izzy declared, and everyone quickly agreed, putting on their headsets, with goggles and headphones attached, and their touchgloves, which allowed them to feel what was happening in the Scape. They all tapped a button on the side of their headpieces and a glowing menu appeared, hovering in the air in front of them, superimposed over the Game Room.

"How about boys against girls?" Nick said with a sly smile.

"Sure," everyone agreed as Nick set up the game.

They all tapped the Glow Ball icon, at which the Game Room promptly faded away, and in its place, filling the empty space in the center of the huge carpeted room, appeared a stone arena with walls slanting away from the ground. Jutting out of stepped pyramids at either end of the field were two small vertical hoops about ten feet in the air, the holes facing each other across the arena. And above it all was a vast starry sky, with the Milky Way like a bright rift cutting across it. It felt almost like being there. And while the adults who grew up with old-fashioned screens still sometimes got vertigo and felt nauseous, Nick, Ethan, Izzy, and Sophie had grown up with VR, so the Scapes seemed almost as real to them as the real world. As the glowing ball appeared in Nick's hand, he declared, "My dad says the new system will blow this one away. It'll be like you're really in the Scape!"

"That's awesome!" Izzy replied. "Now serve the ball already!"

"OK," Nick said. "By the way, Ethan and I are pretty good. Our score is in the 94th percentile for our age, so we'll go easy on you."

"Great, thanks," Sophie said dryly. "Maybe you can teach us some tricks."

Nick served the ball, tossing it up in the air and bumping it gently with the palm of his hand, feeling the pressure of the ball in his touchglove, toward the girls on the other side of the court. Izzy lunged forward and hit the ball hard, straight into the small goal behind the boys. An alarm went off and lights flashed to signal a score, and Sophie and Izzy high-fived while the boys looked dumbstruck. "So that's how it's gonna be, eh?" said Nick, crouching into a more serious position as Sophie got ready to serve the ball.

The two teams turned out to be a pretty even match in the game that resembled a cross between volleyball and basketball, with the hoops positioned differently, and without a net. Over and over, the ball was served and they had some epic volleys going, the glowing orb sometimes banking off the slanting walls in a blur of hands and light. Nick and Izzy both played the front position while Ethan and Sophie played back and to the side. Nick used his patented trick shots and fakes to sneak some goals past the girls, and Ethan was a stalwart defender, making some great saves, but Izzy was relentless and aggressive, often setting the rhythm of the game, the boys struggling to keep up, while Sophie hung back, much more placid and detached, but with a great intuition for knowing where to position herself and timing her hits just right to sneak them past the boys' defenses.

By the time the final buzzer went off, the girls were up six to five. They all panted as they took off their gear, the girls whooping in celebration and the boys grinning sheepishly. "OK, I have to admit," Nick said, "you guys are pretty good."

"Pretty good?" Ethan said incredulously. "They're amazing! What's your guys' team name?"

"We're the Special Unicorns!" Izzy declared triumphantly.

"Are you kidding me?" exclaimed Nick. "I had no idea that was you guys! We're the Wyld Stallyns! Remember we tied in the finals last year?"

"You guys are the Wyld Stallyns?" Sophie laughed. "I somehow thought you would be jocks. Well, nice to finally meet you!"

They all shook hands with mock seriousness, and then grabbed waters out of the mini-fridge and collapsed onto the L-shaped leather couch.

"I think we're all like the Beatles," Nick said, pointing up to the huge photo of the Fab Four above the TV.

"What do you mean?" Izzy asked. Ethan just grinned. Nick's theories were extremely well known to Ethan, who had been listening to them with a mix of interest and amused tolerance ever since they were little kids, when Nick constantly wanted to discuss which Pokémon or Power Ranger each of them was most like.

"Well," Nick said to Izzy, "you're obviously a cross between John, the intense, edgy one, and Paul, the outgoing, cheesy one."

"Hey!" Izzy objected.

"No, he's great! They're two of the greatest singer-songwriters of all time. Paul was the guy who tried to keep the band together when they were breaking up. And he wrote 'Hey Jude' and 'Let It Be.'"

"OK, I admit those are great songs." Izzy seemed mollified.

"Ethan is a cross between John, the deep, intellectual one, and George, the quiet, spiritual one."

"We've discussed this once or twice before," Ethan grinned long-sufferingly.

"I, of course, am a cross between George, the wryly humorous rake, and Paul, the goofy, bossy one."

"That sounds about right," Izzy quipped. "What about Sophie?" Everyone looked at the other girl, whom Ethan thought looked especially lovely with her cheeks flushed and her hair in disarray, smiling a serene, secret smile that reminded him of the Mona Lisa.

"She's Ringo, of course."

"Why do I have to be Ringo?" Sophie asked, looking vaguely wounded. "He's just the drummer!"

"Just the drummer?" Nick retorted. "He's the heart of the band! He was the oldest and most mature member of the group, and his drumming created the feel that helped them become literally the biggest band of all time. Sure, he got the least glory, but he was just as important as the other three in his own way."

"OK," Sophie shrugged, "I guess that does sound kind of like me, though I think I'm also like George. He was really cute, anyway!"

"Alright, I grant that that may be a valid addition to the theory," Nick replied, stroking his chin and smirking.

"Oh my God, you're such a gigantic dork!" Izzy poked Nick playfully in the stomach, and he fell over laughing. "I was thinking we're all kind of like the four character types in AD&D," Izzy continued.

"What's that?" Ethan asked.

"Advanced Dungeons and Dragons!" Izzy replied as if it was the most obvious thing in the world.

"Wait," laughed Nick, "who's a dork?"

"There's nothing dorky about AD&D," Izzy responded with utter conviction, and Sophie gave her a sideways look, half exasperated and half affectionate, while Izzy launched into an explanation of their types. "I'm clearly the warrior," and everyone nodded. There was no point in denying the obvious.

"Sophie is a cleric, kind of like a defender of the faith, because of her calm, steady presence."

"I can see that," Ethan said thoughtfully.

"Ethan is a mage, wizard, whatever you want to call it. He seems to have a lot going on beneath the surface."

"Oh yes, I'm very mysterious," Ethan said.

"Yes," Izzy continued, "and Nick is a rogue. Basically a thief or trickster."

"I mean, I'm not sure about the thief thing," Nick said with a crooked grin, "but trickster sounds about right. Hey!" he sat up suddenly. "Do you guys want to stay for dinner?"

Sophie and Izzy looked at each other, sharing a silent communication. "Sure," said Izzy.

"Sweet! I'll ask my dad if it's OK. I'm sure it will be. I don't think he's said 'no' to me once since the divorce."

"Always look on the bright side of life," chuckled Ethan.

"I guess," said Nick, looking a little sad for a moment, then saying, "who wants carrot sticks and hummus?"

CHAPTER FOUR
DINNER

At dinner in the dining room, surrounded by windows looking out into the trees, the kids were at one end of the long table laughing and joking. Rob Hillman and Christina and David Whitehead were deep in conversation at the other end.

Ethan leaned back from his new friends, smiling broadly, and heard his dad say, "We know it works with adults. The test group within the company has been flawless." David adjusted his glasses and squinted. "But we need to test it on younger minds."

26

Ethan's mom interjected, brushing back a strand of her straight, shoulder-length brown hair. "But we're not sure how the SPECS will interface with brains that are still developing."

"That's true," David replied. By now the other three kids were listening. "But from everything we know, it should be perfectly safe."

"As we're all aware," Christina observed, "tweens and teens are already the biggest Scape users, so we'll have to test the SPECS soon if we want them to be out by next quarter."

"But we don't want the test group to leak information about the SPECS," Rob chimed in, as tan and blond as his son. "We need kids we can trust."

"We'll do it!" Nick called down the table. "Right guys?" His friends nodded excitedly.

"I don't know," said Christina, frowning slightly. "There could be some risk we're not aware of."

"It shouldn't work any differently than it has for us and the others who have been using it for the last year," David reasoned. "The kids' neural networks are certainly more open and fluid than ours, but our simulations don't predict any negative effects on their brain development."

"We're willing to take the risk!" Izzy boldly declared.

"And all of our parents work for the company," Sophie added, "so you won't have to worry about us leaking to the press or other companies."

"We've all basically grown up in the Scapes," Nick said, "so this seems like the obvious next step."

"What do you think, Ethan?" asked David.

"I'd love to be your guinea pig, Dad," Ethan said with a grin. Everyone laughed.

"We won't find smarter or more trustworthy kids, Christina," Rob said, smiling.

"Let's talk about it more tomorrow." David gave his wife a meaningful look.

"OK," said Christina, "we'll discuss it with Izzy and Sophie's parents and let you know what we decide. Now eat your broccoli!" They all laughed.

CHAPTER FIVE
THE BERGSONS

When Izzy got back to the cottage she shared with her mother around dusk, Camille Bergson was in her office, typing away intently at her computer. Her curly brown hair was tied up in a bun, and she had red reading glasses perched on the end of her nose. She looked up when Izzy walked in, and said in a French accent that Izzy barely even noticed, "Hey, Iz! How was your first day of school?"

"Hey, Mom! It was good. Great, actually. I really liked all of my teachers, especially Mr. Gebser. He's amazing."

"Ah, yes," Camille smiled. "He is quite handsome too, no?"

"Yeah, he's pretty dreamy. Maybe you could go on a date with him?" Izzy's parents had split up when she was five, and her father had moved back to France. Her mother had dated a bit, but she was so busy leading the legal team for Rob Hillman's company that she didn't have a lot of time or energy to put into it, and none of her relationships had lasted.

"It's possible," Camille said with a sly grin. "So you had dinner with Nick Hillman's family?"

"Yeah, Nick grew about two inches over the summer, and he seems more mature all of a sudden. His best friend, Ethan, just moved here from Boston, so the four of us hung out all afternoon. I think Ethan and Sophie would be really cute together."

"That sounds perfect, Iz. You and Nick used to be so close."

"Yeah, before the boys decided that girls are gross," Izzy laughed. "I'm glad we're past that phase!" Camille laughed, and then looked back at her screen for a moment and made a few more clicks, finishing up whatever she was working on.

"Mom, can I ask you something?"

"Sure Iz, of course." Camille leaned back in her chair and took off her glasses.

"So Ethan's parents were at dinner, Christina and David Whitehead."

"Oh, yes, of course. I'd forgotten that their son is named Ethan. Their Mentalink technology is incredible. We're lucky that Rob and David are old friends! I think the SPECS are going to be huge for the company."

"That's what I wanted to talk to you about, Mom. They need some kids our age to test the SPECS, and we really want to do it."

"Absolutely not! We have no idea what those things will do to kids' brains. I love this company, but I won't let them use my daughter as their guinea pig!"

"Haven't you tried them?"

"Yes, they're quite wonderful, but . . ."

"Ethan's parents said there's no reason to think it will work any differently for kids than adults. Don't you trust me?"

"It's not that, Iz. It's just that . . . well, you're all I have and if anything ever happened to you . . ."

"Mom, *please*. It sounds like Nick and Ethan's parents are going to let them do it, and knowing Sophie's parents, I'm sure they'll be fine with it. Please don't make me be the only one who can't do it."

"Well, I don't want you to be left out, but how do we know it's safe?"

"Look, Mom, just talk to Ethan's parents. They said they would ask you about it tomorrow. You know me. I'm so responsible. I get straight A's, I help you with chores, I never get in trouble."

"That's true, Iz. You're very mature and I trust you. It just makes me nervous. That's my job as a lawyer, to always think of the worst-case scenario."

"I know, Mom, but can you try to look at this as a mother instead of a lawyer? It would mean so much to me."

Camille looked at her with her best lawyer gaze for a few seconds, and then her will crumbled and she sighed. "Oh, OK. But *be careful!* You have to promise me that if anything strange happens, you'll leave the Scape and tell me immediately."

"Thank you, Mom! Thank you so much! I promise I will! I love you!" Izzy flung her arms around her mother, and then they went to watch an episode of *Gilmore Girls* before bed.

CHAPTER SIX
THE JAMESES

Sophie rode her bike around the back of her family's large wooden house, put the bike in the shed, and went in the back door. Her dad and her eight-year-old brother, Jack, were sitting at the kitchen table drawing. With pale blue eyes and brown hair, they looked strikingly similar, though her father's hair was tied back in a man bun.

"Hey, Soph!" her dad called out. "How was your day?"

Sophie sat down at the table and said, "It was good. Izzy and I have all of our classes together.

We're learning perspective in Art. And we made some new friends. Well, one of them is kind of an old friend. Nick Hillman."

"Ah yes, the boss' son," Jared James said, smiling. He'd been with The Scape since the very beginning. Rob had already been a multi-millionaire from his other companies by the time they met when Sophie was a baby. He had lured Jared away from a top game company, and they had basically created The Scape between the two of them. They had become close friends over the last decade.

"And the other one is Ethan Whitehead."

"Oh right, Christina and David's son!" He looked at his daughter with a grin. "Do I detect a little crush?"

"Dad!" Sophie blushed and hid her face in her hands, and Jack looked up from his drawing of a spaceship and sang, "Sophie's got a boyfriend, Sophie's got a boyfriend."

"I do not, twerp!" They all laughed.

"What's so funny, you three?" Sophie's mom, Heather, walked into the room, looking perfect as always in her yoga clothes and her blond ponytail, her ever-present pink yoga mat under her arm. "Hey, sweetie, how was your first day of school?" She smiled, but Sophie had a feeling that she disapproved of her hair, still messy from playing Glow Ball.

"It was good. I liked my classes and we made some new friends."

"That's great, sweetie." She smiled her perfect smile. "Well, I'm off to the advanced class. Love you!" She kissed Sophie and Jack on the tops of their heads, gave Jared a peck on the cheek, and left.

Jared and Jack went back to drawing. "Dad?" Sophie said after a minute lost in thought, absently combing her fingers through her hair.

"Yeah, Soph?"

"Nick and Ethan's parents were talking at dinner about how they need some kids to test the SPECS. We all want to do it. Is that OK?"

"Oh, that's a great idea! I can't wait for you to try the new Scapes!"

"Thanks, Daddy! You're the best!" And she launched out of her chair and gave her dad a huge hug. Jack, not wanting to miss out, piled on, and they all hugged and laughed.

CHAPTER SEVEN
SPECS

After school the next day, the four friends rode their bikes through the park back to Nick's house, but thankfully there was no sign of Milo, Stefan, and the Peterson twins. Blue greeted them, and then the kids went down to the Game Room to hang out.

Even though Nick's dad worked a ridiculous amount, he almost always made it home in time for a late dinner with his son, and Blue sometimes joined them. In the middle of a conversation about their favorite bands, they heard Rob's voice call down the stairs. "Hey, kids, come on up! I've got some news!"

"Wow, I don't think he's ever been home this early!" said Nick, and they all jumped up off the couch and trotted upstairs into the kitchen.

Rob was standing at the white marble island, chatting with Blue while she folded the laundry at the kitchen table. The kids sat down on stools at the island. "So we talked with your parents this morning, Izzy and Sophie," began Rob in an amused tone. "It sounds like you gave them the hard sell last night."

"Yeah," said Izzy, "my mom wasn't so sure at first, but I talked her around."

"Well, you learned from the best," Rob chuckled. "Your mom is a great lawyer. I'm glad she's on my side. I certainly wouldn't want to go up against her in court!"

"Try being her daughter!" Izzy sighed dramatically.

"And your parents seem fine with it, Sophie. They say they trust you completely."

Sophie smiled. "I think my dad is mostly just excited to share his new creations with me!"

"That sounds like Jared," Rob laughed.

"So what did you decide, Dad?" Nick asked.

Rob looked at them all for a moment with a searching gaze, and then reached into his messenger bag and brought out what looked like four white sunglass cases. "We've decided to let you all try the SPECS." There was an excited murmur from the kids. "We won't be able to see exactly what you're doing in the Scapes, but we'll be closely monitoring your brainwaves through the devices. So you all have to promise to be careful, and let us know if anything unusual happens."

"We will, Dad!" said Nick, and the others agreed.

Rob handed them all a case, the hard plastic cool to the touch, and said, "You probably already know this, but I'm going to tell you anyway. SPECS stands for Sensory Perception Emulation Control Systems." The SPECS looked exactly like black Wayfarer sunglasses. "Ethan's parents developed the Mentalink technology over the last few years, and we've been working hard to streamline the devices so they fit inside normal looking glasses."

"These are so cool!" breathed Izzy.

"I wouldn't even know there was a computer inside just by looking at it," said Sophie, closely examining her device.

"They aren't just computers," Ethan said. "They're massively parallel quantum processors paired with the Mentalink technology, which uses quantum entanglement to transfer a constant stream of huge amounts of data between the SPECS and the user's cortex. So there's no energy beaming into your head, which would basically cook your brain. Instead, the link creates an instantaneous resonance between your brain's atoms and the atoms in the processors. So, in a way, the SPECS become almost like a part of your brain."

"What happens if they break or fall off or something?" asked Sophie.

"The link just dissolves," Ethan responded, "and you slip out of the Scape, kind of like waking up in the middle of a dream."

"That's exactly right," said Rob. "Looks like someone has been paying attention to what Mom and Dad are up to!"

"It's all they talk about!" Ethan laughed. "I'm just happy we finally get to try it," he said, glancing at Nick.

"Yeah, Dad," said Nick. "Thanks for trusting us. We know this is a big deal and we won't let you down."

"I know you won't, Nicky," said Rob, putting his hand affectionately on his son's shoulder. "Now you kids have fun!"

CHAPTER EIGHT
THE SLOPES

Back in the Game Room, they all flung themselves down on the couch and put on their SPECS, tapping a button next to their temples to turn them on. "Wow, these are much lighter than the old gear!" Izzy exclaimed. "You can barely tell they're even there!"

A menu not very different from the one in the old system popped up in front of them, superimposed over the Game Room. "So what do you guys want to do?" Nick asked.

"How about skiing?" suggested Sophie. Everyone agreed, and they all tapped on the Slopes icon.

The room faded away, and they found themselves standing at the top of a mountain dressed in full skiing gear, a vast snowy landscape spread out below them. The crisp air bit at their cheeks, warmed just the right amount by the bright sun. "This is incredible!" cried Ethan, who could feel the sting of cold air in his lungs and the ski boots snug on his feet.

"It feels like we're really here!" Izzy shouted.

"They've really done it," Nick breathed in an awed tone. "I mean, they said it felt real, but this isn't *like* being here. We're *here!*"

"I know," Sophie mused. "The idea that our bodies are back in the Game Room is really strange." She gave a shiver that was only partly due to the cold. "It feels like we've just transported to a different place. This is going to change the world!" Everyone was quiet for a moment, taking it all in.

Then Izzy broke the silence. "This slope looks amazing. Let's go!" She pushed off down the hill, and they all followed her, both stunned and thrilled by the sheer reality of the experience as they flew down the slope, the wind rushing in their ears.

Ethan had gone skiing with his parents almost every year up in Vermont since he could walk. He'd always loved the little side paths that led off through the pine trees, so he took the first one he saw leading off to the right while his friends zoomed on down the main slope. He rounded a corner, and came to a little jump at full speed. He was a pretty experienced skier, but he was distracted by the mind-blowing newness of the experience, and he miscalculated and wiped out, landing in a soft bank, feeling the icy snow on his neck, seeping in at the top of his parka. He lay there for a minute, just feeling the snow on his skin. Then he sat up, took off one of his gloves, and scooped a handful of the pure, white powder into his mouth. It tasted just like the fresh snow scraped from the top of their fence that they made ice cream with growing up.

Ethan heard the excited whooping and shouting of his friends growing fainter in the distance. He pushed himself up, brushed the snow off his clothes, and crunched over to where his skis had landed when they flew off his boots in the crash. As he bent down to put his boot back in its ski, he sensed something out of the corner of his eye, and turned to peer into the trees. About twenty feet up and over, he saw what looked like the mouth of a cave, but it was glowing blue and flickering, as if it was a glitch in the system. He tried to look at it more closely, to get it to hold still, but his eyes kept sliding away from it so that he couldn't quite take it in all at once. He thought it must just be something wrong with the code. But Ethan had a strange sense that there was something important in that cave, something that tickled the back of his mind like a forgotten dream.

He put down the ski and crunched toward the cave to take a closer look, but after a few steps, it winked out of existence, and in its place was just more snow. He stared at the spot where the cave had been for a minute, and then figuring it was just a glitch, he crunched back to his skis. But as he knocked the snow off his boots and wedged them into the bindings, he couldn't shake a strong desire to know what was beyond that opening. Surely it was just something in the program that needed tweaking? But why then did he feel the hairs on the back of his neck standing up? It must just be the cold, he thought. The cold that's only in my brain, he smiled to himself.

With his skis back on, he continued down the path, bursting over a jump out onto the main slope. This time he landed with satisfying precision, and he sped after his friends who were now specks far below.

When he got to the bottom of the run, he saw his friends' skis leaned up against the side of a small lodge, so he did the same, and made his way indoors. Nick, Sophie, and Izzy were all sitting in front of a roaring fire with their boots off, sipping cups of what smelled like hot chocolate. "Where have you been?" asked Nick. "We were starting to get worried."

"Oh, I wiped out on a jump on a side trail."

"Oh, bummer," said Izzy.

"Taste this hot chocolate!" Sophie said, holding out a steaming mug for him. "They were sitting on the table when we came in."

Ethan plopped down next to her, feeling deliciously exhausted after the long run. The blazing fire radiated a pleasant warmth after the cold outside, and he took the mug in his hands. He still couldn't quite believe they were in Virtual Reality. The old Scapes were pretty convincing, but this was a whole other level. If he didn't already know that he was in a Scape, he didn't think he would have been able to say if this experience was virtual or real.

"Take a sip," Sophie said, looking at him expectantly. He did, and the thick, hot drink slightly burned his tongue, the warmth spreading through his body as he swallowed the delicious liquid.

"This is really incredible," said Izzy. "I can't believe this isn't real. It just feels *so real.*"

"I know, it's really crazy," said Nick. "Go parents! It's pretty amazing that we're the first kids to ever experience this."

"Seriously," Ethan grinned. "By the way, I think there might be a glitch in the code. I saw some kind of glowing cave, but then it disappeared."

"Really?" said Izzy. "I didn't see anything like that. We should probably tell our parents."

"Maybe we shouldn't," said Nick. "What if they decide our brains are too unformed or something and they don't let us back in here? It doesn't sound like it was a big deal, was it, Ethan?"

"I don't know. I guess not," he replied.

"I mean, what harm can it do?" Nick continued. "If anything goes wrong, we can just exit the Scape, right?"

"OK," said Izzy hesitantly, "but if something like this happens again, I think we should tell them."

They all sat looking at the fire and sipping their cocoa for a few more minutes before they put their fingers to their temples, where the button would be on the SPECS if they were wearing them in the Scape, and the lodge dissolved into the Game Room. They all looked at each other, just savoring the momentous experience. Then Ethan realized that his tongue still felt slightly tender from the hot chocolate, like an echo of the feeling. And even though they had technically been sitting on the couch for the last hour or two, his body felt like he had been skiing. "I think I'm actually going to be sore tomorrow!" he said, and they all laughed.

CHAPTER NINE
SPACE BATTLE

The next day after school, they all hurried back to Nick's house to try another Scape. This time they chose Space Battle, where they would each pilot a small fighter ship against enemy ships in an asteroid field.

As soon as they entered the Scape, Ethan could feel the weightlessness of space even though he was strapped into the cockpit, and he ran his hands over the cool, smooth metal and plastic of the ship's controls. He tried a few maneuvers, looping around with his friends in their sleek grey ships, firing his lasers. "Hey, watch where you're pointing that thing!" Sophie laughed through the comm.

"Check it out!" Nick said, and he punched the thrusters directly toward the nearest small asteroid, sharply banking up and to the left just before he smashed into it.

"Be careful, you maniac!" Ethan quipped.

"Here come the enemy fighters!" called Izzy excitedly. Ethan looked to the right and saw about a dozen angular black ships swooping toward them menacingly. The friends all scrambled in different directions to avoid getting blasted, Ethan banking straight up and off between two asteroids on a collision course in front of him. A second after he passed between them, he saw the giant space rocks crash together with a huge force in his rear monitor. He took a deep breath, his heart beating furiously. "This is insane!" he called out to his friends.

"I know!" Nick responded.

"I got one!" Izzy yelled joyfully, and Ethan saw a brief flash of orange light in the distance off to the left. He looked in his rear monitor again and saw two of the black fighters coming after him around the two asteroids that had collided, now broken into a hundred pieces flying off in every direction. He swooped and dove through the oncoming asteroids as laser blasts narrowly missed him, but he couldn't shake his pursuers.

This obviously wasn't working, so he decided to try a new tactic. He saw a larger asteroid, almost a tiny moon, looming off to his right, and he punched the thrusters toward it, the enemy hot on his tail. He bobbed and weaved his way toward the big asteroid, managing to avoid a direct hit from the lasers, though his wings got singed a few times. And then he was just above the surface of the rough, pitted orb, banking sharply toward its horizon. Scanning the surface desperately, he burst out over a shallow canyon and, with reflexes honed by years of playing games like this, slammed on the brake thrusters and dropped down into the canyon. A second later, the two ships zoomed over him and he trained his sight on them, squeezing the trigger expertly. They were two direct hits, both ships exploding in orange flames.

He lay back against the headrest, closed his eyes, and just breathed for a few seconds, his heart pounding. When he opened his eyes, he saw blue light off at the other end of the canyon, and he tapped the thrusters to investigate. When he got closer, he saw that it was a flickering cave, glowing blue like the one he had seen the day before on the Slopes. It looked just big enough to fit his ship, and he felt an overwhelming urge to see what was in the cave, so he nudged the ship gently in that direction. But when he was a second or two away, he sensed something above him, and he turned his head up just in time to see one of the enemy ships fire a laser directly at him. The last thing he saw before the Scape dissolved back into the Game Room was the orange flames from his exploding ship.

It was like waking up from the most realistic dream imaginable. Or maybe this was the dream, and that was reality, he chuckled to himself. But really, it would have been impossible to tell which world was real and which was virtual if he didn't already know.

He took off his SPECS. His friends were still in the Scape, but there was no sign of what they were doing. Then he noticed that behind Nick's glasses, his eyes were closed, but they were moving like he was having an intense dream. Ethan looked over at Sophie, and he felt his heart pounding again for a different reason than when he had been in the Scape. Suddenly, her eyes opened, and she drew in a big breath, whipped off her glasses, and looked directly at Ethan, who realized he was still staring at her. "What?" she asked, smiling.

Ethan looked away, feeling his cheeks flush. "Nothing," he said. "Just wondering how you guys were doing."

"We won the battle! What happened to you?"

"I destroyed two of them, but then I wasn't paying attention and one got me."

"Oh, sorry," she said sympathetically.

"It's OK," he said. "I saw that glitch again. The Cave."

"Weird. Did it look the same?"

"Yeah, exactly the same. But . . ."

"What?"

"Well, it's strange, but both times I've seen the Cave, I've had this urge to go into it, like it's calling me."

"What do you think that means?" She looked thoughtful.

"I have no idea," he shrugged. Just then, Nick and Izzy both took off their SPECS, smiling.

"That ruled!" Nick exclaimed. "You were amazing, Izzy!"

"Thanks, buddy," she beamed. "You were pretty good yourself."

"I saw that one guy take you down, Ethan," said Nick. "Don't worry, I avenged you."

"Oh, my hero," Ethan said dryly.

"Ethan saw that cave glitch again," Sophie told the other two.

"Weird," Nick mused. "Did anything else happen with it?"

"No," Ethan replied. "They got me before I could check it out."

"We should tell our parents," Izzy said, looking slightly worried.

"But we're having so much fun!" Nick objected. "If we tell them, they'll probably want to take the SPECS away to study them or something. Can we please just wait a few more days?"

"OK, fine," said Izzy grudgingly. "But if he sees it again, I'm telling them."

"OK, jeez. Spoilsport."

CHAPTER TEN
QUESTIONS

That night, Ethan was having dinner with his parents back at their Spanish-style ranch house, which his dad jokingly referred to as the Hacienda. "So how are you kids liking the SPECS so far?" his dad asked.

"They're incredible! I can't believe how real it is. How is it possible that my legs are sore from skiing when I was sitting on the couch the whole time?"

"Great question," Ethan's mom said in her professor voice. "We were pretty surprised when that happened too. We don't completely understand it yet, but our best guess is that, because the SPECS essentially act as a part of your nervous system, your body thinks that it's really doing whatever it seems like you're doing in the Scape."

"So what happens if you get hurt?"

"We've tested this a lot," his dad chimed in, "and what we've found is that injuries only leave a faint trace, so a deep cut would just show up as a little scratch, or a broken bone would leave a mild bruise. So even if you got seriously injured in the Scape, it would only show up as a minor echo in the real world."

"If I do push-ups in the Scape, will that give me muscles?" Ethan asked.

"It would eventually," his mom replied, "but not nearly as quickly as doing them in the real world."

"Are you thinking about starting to work out?" his dad asked with a smile.

"Maybe," said Ethan, an image of Sophie coming unbidden into his mind. "What if someone in the real world tries to mess with you while you're in the Scape?" Ethan asked.

"The SPECS automatically shut off if someone comes too close to the user," his dad answered, "or if something is moving toward them quickly."

"Like if someone throws a ball at you?" Ethan asked.

"That's right," his dad answered. "But even though there are safeguards, it's still a good idea to always use the SPECS in a safe, controlled setting."

"So has anything unusual happened?" asked his mom with her penetrating gaze.

"Why?" Ethan stalled, remembering Nick's insistence on not telling their parents. "Has anything shown up in my brainwaves?"

"No," his mom looked at him searchingly. "It's all been normal. Is there anything we should know?"

"No," Ethan lied, feeling bad about deceiving his parents, but also wanting to keep his promise to his friends. "Nothing." He took a big bite of curry so he wouldn't have to answer any more questions, and his parents went back to talking about work.

CHAPTER ELEVEN
ORC CAVERNS

The next day after school, they went straight down to the Game Room to try another Scape called Orc Caverns, a *Lord of the Rings*-style adventure. Tapping the buttons on their SPECS, the Game Room faded away, and they found themselves in a small, damp cavern, with torches burning in brackets on the walls, and tunnels leading off in three different directions.

"Hey, you look cool!" Nick said to Izzy, who was dressed in light silver armor, with a warrior's longsword sticking up out of a scabbard on her back.

"You do too," she smiled back at Nick, who was wearing a tunic, trousers, a cloak, and a rakish hat, all in various shades of brown, with at least eight knives stowed on different parts of his body. Sophie looked radiant in the white robes of a cleric, with a simple silver circlet holding back her dark red hair, and a silver dagger in a sheath at her thin silver belt. Ethan found himself holding a gnarled mage's staff, and he saw that he was wearing all black, including a long cloak, with a shortsword strapped to his black leather belt.

"Did you program in our character types, Nick?" Sophie asked.

"No, I didn't," he replied.

"Then how did it match us with the types Izzy was talking about the other day?" wondered Ethan.

"I don't know," said Nick. "Maybe the SPECS can read our minds or something?"

"Maybe," said Ethan. "The SPECS are technically part of our brains, so I guess that makes sense."

"Shhh, I hear something!" whispered Izzy excitedly. They all went quiet, and they could hear the faint pounding of boots and someone barking what sounded like orders in a guttural language none of them had ever heard before.

"What should we do?" asked Sophie.

"Let's go fight!" said Izzy, and she jogged off into one of the tunnels toward the noise. The other three looked at each other, shrugged, and ran after her.

They rounded a corner and found themselves at the opening of a huge cavern, at one end of an ancient-looking stone bridge stretching across an abyss that looked like it went down forever. About halfway across the bridge, there was a large group of tall, muscular humanoid creatures with greenish-grey skin and bestial features marching along. "Orcs!" shouted Izzy gleefully, at which the creatures looked in their direction, and with a terrifying roar, began to charge.

"Oh my God!" shouted Nick.

"Hold your ground!" shouted Izzy, naturally assuming the role of battle leader.

"I'm not sure about this, Iz!" warned Sophie.

"It'll be OK, Soph. Just use your magic," Izzy threw back over her shoulder as she drew her longsword. "I've been waiting for this my whole life!"

Ethan, drawing his own blade, felt something whiz past his ear, and he froze for a moment, stunned. Then with a loud thunk, an arrow, almost like a small spear, smacked hard into Izzy's breastplate, knocking her off her feet. "Are you OK?" Nick said, quickly helping her up.

"Yeah, I'm fine," she said, looking slightly disoriented.

"Maybe we shouldn't try to fight them head on," said Ethan urgently as the howling horde of about two dozen orcs, each one about eight feet tall, charged toward them, about ten seconds away.

"OK," said Izzy grudgingly. "Let's retreat and find a place to ambush them!" And she led the group back into the tunnel, back past the small cavern where they had started, and down the tunnel to the left. They ran for a minute, the stomping, growling orcs not far behind, and Nick observed, "I'm not sure this is my favorite Scape. It's a little too real!"

"We just have to find a ledge or something where we can get an advantage!" Izzy declared confidently as they rounded a corner and almost ran into a wall.

"A dead end!" shouted Sophie. "What should we do?"

"I guess we have to make our stand here," said Izzy, looking less confident, even a little grim.

They could hear the horde quickly approaching, and they all readied their weapons. "I don't know," Nick said. "Maybe we should just tap out. This is nuts."

Ethan, feeling a panic starting to build, was about to agree with Nick when he saw a flash of blue light out of the corner of his eye, and there was the glowing, flickering opening he had already seen twice in a little recess off to the side. "The Cave!" he shouted, and his friends all looked over, the orcs about to hurtle around the bend by the sound of it. "Follow me!" he yelled, and plunged through the shimmering portal.

CHAPTER TWELVE
THE PLEROMA

Ethan was falling into blackness, twisting in a strange, unfamiliar way, like slipping through a crack just at the edge of his vision. And after what could have been aeons or a second, he found himself standing on a platform in a huge space. Staircases stretched off in various directions, but in ways that didn't make sense, so that a flight of stairs that went up from the platform he was standing on somehow ended up on a platform below him. It reminded him of a print by M.C. Escher his dad had on the wall of his study. And there was a sense of vastness, like he was seeing everything through a fish-eye lens, taking in a wider view than he ever had before. It was both exhilarating and disorienting, like he suddenly had a sixth sense as real as sight, sound, touch, taste, and smell, though he didn't know what to call it. What was this place? And where were his friends?

He took a step toward the nearest staircase leading up/down, and the world tilted around him in a bizarre way. He went down on one knee and closed his eyes, trying to regain his sense of balance, his hand steadying himself on the floor.

When he opened his eyes, still in a kneeling position, a radiant being hovered in front of him. It was a tall, ageless woman in flowing white robes with long white hair, rippling in a wind that he couldn't feel, emanating a white light that made him squint and avert his eyes. "Hello, Ethan," she said in a soft, melodious voice that seemed to come from inside his head as much as from her lips, and filled the space like a gentle caress.

"Who are you?" Ethan managed to get out, his voice sounding small in his ears. "What is this place?"

"Welcome to the Pleroma, Ethan. Many of your kind have been here before you, but you and your friends are the first from your world to come in this way, through a Gateway. We are pleased to see you." Her voice filled his mind, touching something deep inside of him, something he only ever recalled being vaguely aware of in dreams.

"A Gateway? You mean the Cave? Are my friends OK?"

"Your friends are fine, Ethan. They are all seeing the aspect of the Pleroma that will allow them to begin to understand this domain."

"What do you mean? Is this part of the Scape?"

"No, Ethan. What you call the Scape is the threshold to the Gateway."

"So, what? Is this like a glitch in the software?" But even as he said it, he knew that this place and this being were much more than a programming mistake, and the being's laugh, like a tinkle of distant bells, confirmed his feeling.

"No, Ethan," she smiled. "The Pleroma has always been here. It has always been with you." And then suddenly she grew serious. "But it is not yet time for you to understand this domain. We need your help. You and your friends have arrived just in time."

"You need our help? How can we possibly help you?"

"Your world is in crisis, Ethan. And our worlds are connected. What happens in your world affects ours."

"I don't understand," Ethan said, shaking his head, starting to feel dizzy from the vastness of the space and the profound strangeness of the experience. Then a thought occurred to him. "Am I stuck here?" Ethan asked with a sense of rising panic. "Will I be able to go back to my family, my friends?"

"You can leave whenever you wish, Ethan. You can leave this domain the same way you leave the Scapes, at the touch of a button." Ethan breathed a sigh of relief. "And it is almost time for you to depart. But before you go, I want to give you something." She pulled an ancient-looking leather-bound book out of her robes, and presented it to Ethan, still kneeling, who carefully reached out and took the book with both hands. On the cover, embossed in silver letters, was written *The Book of Eris*, and there was a symbol, also in silver, that looked like a plus sign with a loop for the left arm.

"Are you Eris?" Ethan asked, squinting into the woman's eyes, which seemed to pull him into their dizzying depths, so that he had to look away.

"That is one of my names," the shining woman said, smiling. "Your astronomers finally discovered my planet a short time ago."

"Your planet? What do you mean? Are we on a different planet?"

"Not exactly, Ethan," she said with a kindly air. "But that is enough for now. Study the book, and I will explain more the next time you visit."

"Next time?"

"Oh yes, I will see you soon, Ethan." The woman spun around, and a bright flash radiated from her, so bright that Ethan had to close his eyes.

CHAPTER THIRTEEN
GIFTS

When Ethan opened his eyes, he was back in the Game Room. He took off his SPECS, and saw that the others were doing the same, all looking dazed, staring off into space, as if they hadn't completely returned. He knew how they felt.

They all sat silently like that for a minute, but then, slowly, they started to tell what they had seen in the Pleroma beyond the Cave. Izzy had found herself at the mouth of a volcano, meeting a being made of fire. "She said I would probably know her as Pluto or Hades," Izzy said, "but she preferred to be called

Kali. She was so powerful! It was hard to even look at her."

"Eris was the same way," said Ethan. "Did Kali give you anything? Eris gave me a book, but it doesn't seem to have made it back to the real world."

"She gave me a green sword that was way cooler than the one I had in the caverns," said Izzy. "What about you, Nick?"

"I was in the mountains, and there was lightning but no rain. Then this funny guy appeared who said he was Prometheus, but that astronomers had misnamed his planet as Uranus."

"What does that mean?" Ethan wondered. "Are they aliens from different planets in the Solar System?"

"I have no idea," said Nick, "but he gave me a really old-looking gold coin with his face on one side and this symbol on the other," and he traced it in the air.

"That was on the cover of my book!" exclaimed Ethan.

"And it was on the pommel of my sword!" Izzy said excitedly.

"You guys," said Sophie, examining her SPECS carefully. "Look at this." And she pointed to a tiny mark next to the button. They all leaned in, and saw that it was the symbol! "I'm pretty sure this wasn't here before," said Sophie, as they all looked at their SPECS and saw that the symbol was on all of them. "I was underwater in a coral reef," Sophie said, "and then Neptune, or Poseidon, appeared, but he said I could call him Vishnu, and he gave me a pendant with this symbol on it. I think it's a kind of ampersand, a symbol for 'and.'"

"How do you know that?" Ethan asked, impressed.

"Oh, my dad's really into stuff like that," Sophie responded.

"So what is all this?" asked Izzy. "Is this part of the Scape, a weird surprise left for us by our parents?"

"I don't think so," said Ethan. "I don't think our parents could have planned this, and Eris told me it wasn't a glitch. I think the SPECS somehow opened the Cave, which Eris called a Gateway, to another world. She said other people have been there before."

"Yeah, Prometheus said the same thing," Nick said. "So are they, like, gods or something?"

"I don't know," Ethan responded, "but maybe we can find out. Eris told me to read the book. Maybe it's in the SPECS somehow?"

"Yeah," said Izzy. "Kali told me to practice with the sword."

"Vishnu told me to meditate on the pendant," Sophie said thoughtfully.

Nick laughed. "Prometheus just told me to flip the coin and try my luck. And then he winked at me!"

"This is crazy, you guys. Should we tell our parents now?" Izzy wondered.

"I really don't think we should," Nick said forcefully. "They'll definitely take the SPECS away."

"I agree," said Sophie quietly. "This feels like it was meant to be. They chose us, not our parents."

"Yeah," agreed Ethan. "This seems like a huge deal, and I think we're supposed to keep it a secret for now."

Everyone nodded, and just then, Blue called down the stairs, "Hey kids, it's getting late!" The friends all put their SPECS away, said their goodbyes, and rode their bikes home, their heads filled with strange visions.

CHAPTER FOURTEEN
THE BOOK OF ERIS

That night after dinner, Ethan went up to his room. He sat on his bed, and took out his SPECS, examining the tiny ampersand symbol next to the button. Eris had told him to read the book, but how?

He put on the SPECS and pressed the button, the menu springing to life in the air in front of him. He scrolled down with a casual flick of his wrist, and at the bottom of the menu was a new icon that hadn't been there before. It was a leather-bound book with silver writing and the ampersand embossed on the cover. His hand trembling slightly, with fear or excitement he wasn't sure, he tapped the icon and his room faded away to blackness. And there he floated in the void for what could have been a moment or an eternity.

Then, suddenly, a point of light popped into existence off in the distance, exploding outward with unbelievable force. *This must be the Big Bang!* he thought. He watched as the expanding sphere of pure energy approached him, and then engulfed him. It plunged him into a swirling chaos of light and heat, which he could see and feel, though it didn't blind or burn him as it would have if he had really been there to witness the beginning of the universe.

Flash. Now he was standing on a rocky planet. Great oceans and fiery volcanoes warred for dominance as the land writhed and cracked, mountains and seas forming and melting away. He could feel time moving faster now, ten times as quickly as it had been before, like a slow-moving river beginning to ease toward falls. He looked down at a small tide pool and was somehow able to see tiny single-celled organisms busily devouring energy from the environment and dividing over and over, filling the turbulent waters.

Flash. Time was moving ten times faster again as he watched the first amphibious creatures pushing themselves out of the water onto the rocks, their eyes searching as they escaped the predators of the deep in this strange new world.

Flash. He stood in a thick jungle, and time was moving ten times faster again, accelerating everything. There were creatures that looked like apes or chimpanzees swinging in the trees above him, whooping loudly in what seemed like a frantic, joyful dance.

Flash. Time was moving ten times faster again, and he saw what looked like primal humans dancing naked around a bonfire, their voices raised in an ancient, rhythmic, wordless song.

Flash. Again, time was moving ten times faster, and he saw men and women, clothed in animal skins, sitting around a fire. An old woman, wearing a headdress made of bones and feathers, was telling a story, motioning broadly with her arms as unfamiliar words poured from her lips, the others listening attentively.

Flash. Ten times faster, rushing down the rapids, Ethan saw thousands of men and women hauling massive stones toward a half-finished pyramid, and people with chisels hammering away at smaller standing stones, carving elaborate symbols that must have been early writing. Looking out past the workers, he saw a city beside a river stretching off into the distance.

Flash. Ten times faster, the pace growing almost unbearable. Ethan saw an old Middle Eastern man in robes carrying two stone tablets down a mountain path to the people waiting below. *Moses,* whispered Eris' voice. A middle-aged Greek woman playing a lyre and singing to a young woman with flowers woven into her long black hair. *Sappho.* An old Chinese man scratching characters by candlelight onto a scroll. *Confucius.* A young Indian man meditating beneath a large, gnarled tree, its arms stretching in all directions. *Buddha.* An old man in a toga speaking to men lying on couches, drinking wine and laughing. *Socrates.* A young man with kind eyes speaking to twelve men sitting at his feet, gazing up at him adoringly. *Jesus.* A middle-aged man with a turban and a dark beard kneeling on a rug at the mouth of a cave, his face turned upward, radiant. *Mohammed.*

Flash. Ten times faster, hurtling hysterically toward some unseen precipice. A man with a large nose and funny mushroom-shaped hair intently studying a device made of metal rings nested inside one another, with markings depicting the locations of the planets. *Nicolaus Copernicus.* A man with a long white beard and hooded eyes gazing through a telescope at the night sky. *Galileo Galilei.* A young man with long wavy hair and a sharp nose sitting beneath an apple tree, deep in thought. *Isaac Newton.* A young woman in a Victorian dress and elaborate curls peering at a large machine with columns upon columns of cogs and cranks. *Ada Lovelace.* A young man with long sideburns and a prominent brow standing at the bow of a large wooden ship, watching hundreds of dolphins leaping in the waves. *Charles*

Darwin. A handsome young man with a mustache and short curly hair sitting at a desk in a large bustling office, watching the window washers working outside, lost in thought. *Albert Einstein.* An older man with a white beard and a younger man with round wire-rim glasses sitting in armchairs by a fire, deep in conversation. *Sigmund Freud and Carl Jung.* Two young men in different garages, one intense with dark hair and one cheerful with large glasses, both building something with wires and circuits. *Steve Jobs and Bill Gates.*

Flash. And the stream of images faded away, leaving Ethan staring at the wall. He slowly took off the SPECS and fell back on the bed, his head spinning. He felt like he had just read a thousand books about religion and science and philosophy and technology. It was too much to take in all at once, and his brain couldn't focus on the huge amount of information that it had just absorbed. But he felt like it was there at the edge of his mind, a vast pool of knowledge waiting to be tapped.

Exhausted, Ethan closed his eyes and slept.

CHAPTER FIFTEEN
LUNCH

The next day at lunch, the four friends were sitting at their usual table in the cafeteria, leaning in and talking in low voices. Ethan, who wasn't feeling hungry, had just finished telling them as much as he could about his experience with *The Book of Eris* the night before.

"So you saw the whole history of the world?" Nick said attentively through a mouthful of pepperoni pizza.

"Not exactly the history of the world, like wars and kings and stuff. More like the history of ideas, the way animals and people have thought about things. And it wasn't exactly like seeing it. It was more like being inside of it, almost experiencing it from their perspective. I feel like I understand so much more than I did before, but I don't know how to explain it all. It's like a huge ocean I can feel behind me, but I can't quite turn around and look at it."

"That's amazing!" said Izzy. "I learned how to do martial arts."

"Fighting?" Nick asked, his mouth still full.

"Sort of, but it's more like dance, or chess. I never knew how much thought went into focusing and channeling your chi."

"What's chi?" asked Nick.

"It's like your life-force. In the martial arts, there are all different ways of using your chi, but what the greatest martial artists have understood is that fighting an enemy is only the lowest level of the art. Mastering yourself, both mentally and physically, is the art's real essence."

"Wow, you sound like an expert!" said Ethan.

"Yeah, I feel like I know all of these movements in my body that I haven't even tried yet," she said, punching the air experimentally. Then she smiled and looked at Nick. "Maybe we can try some moves later!"

"OK, Sensei Wu, but you'll have to go easy on me," Nick said with a grin. He had a bit of tomato sauce on his chin, which Izzy wiped away with her napkin, Nick looking half embarrassed and half pleased.

"What did the pendant do, Sophie?" Ethan asked.

Sophie looked thoughtful, and then said, "It's hard to explain. It wasn't a download of knowledge or a skill. It was more like I was swimming in different wavelengths of light, different vibrations of reality. And I could sense so many beings, not just humans or animals, but all kinds of spirits or something stretching out through the whole universe. They were all so different, feeling things that I've never felt before, things I couldn't even have imagined. But they were all one too. Like I said, it's hard to explain."

"Sounds like somebody had a mystical experience," said Nick wryly. "My mom's always going to spiritual retreats and having these 'profound' revelations. But she always kind of sounds like she's pretending. She *is* an actor, after all. This seems different."

"Yeah, it was pretty incredible," Sophie mused. "There's just so much out there—or maybe in there—that we haven't experienced. But after I felt all those beings, the main thing I felt was just a deep sense of peace." Her face glowed serenely as she recalled the feeling, and then she turned to Nick. "How about you?" she asked.

"Me?" Nick said. "Oh, I spent some time with quite a cast of characters, like seeing a bunch of interrelated stories from the inside. There were Coyote and Raven, Loki and Anansi, Lilith and Sinbad, Odysseus and Brer Rabbit, Puck and Maui. They're all characters who know how to get things done, how to cross boundaries and find the connections that other people miss. A bunch of tricksters, basically," he said with a grin.

"I should have known," laughed Izzy. "Our very own court jester!"

"Guilty as charged," Nick laughed. "But tricksters have done some pretty awesome things. Prometheus is one of them, and he stole fire from the gods and gave it to humanity."

"That's true," said Ethan. "But wasn't he punished for it? Didn't Zeus chain him to a rock and send an eagle to eat his liver every day?"

"Ew!" Izzy exclaimed.

"Yeah," responded Nick. "Well, as the great sage Snoop Dogg says, you gotta pay the cost to be the boss."

"Who's Snoop Dogg?" Izzy asked.

"I have no idea," Nick admitted sheepishly. "It's just something my dad says," and they all laughed. Nick pulled his SPECS case out of his bag, took the "glasses" out, and started examining them. "These things are so cool," he mused.

"Hey," Sophie said, looking across the cafeteria, "it's the Peterson twins." Everyone turned and saw Connor and Abigail Peterson sitting at a table over in the high school area. They were staring at them and whispering to each other, Connor scowling and Abigail smiling like a fox about to raid the hen house.

Nick quickly put the SPECS away. "Let's get out of here," he said. Everyone agreed, so they put their lunch trays on the racks and made a hasty exit into the crowded hallway. Ethan was looking back over his shoulder toward the Peterson twins when he felt something ram into him, and he was knocked to the floor.

"Watch where you're going, freak," said Milo Spencer, the gaunt boy with stringy black hair.

"What the hell?" Nick called out as Milo walked away, laughing, other kids standing around watching the commotion. Izzy gave Ethan a hand up while Sophie picked his bag up off the floor.

"You OK?" Sophie said as she handed him the bag.

"Yeah," Ethan said, brushing his pants off. "I'm fine."

"I can't believe *he* called *you* a freak," Izzy said.

"Yeah, has he looked in the mirror lately?" Nick said. "He looks like Professor Snape's creepier younger brother." They all laughed, but their mood was uneasy as they walked to their next class.

CHAPTER SIXTEEN
THE CONCRETION OF TIME

Later that afternoon in Intro to Philosophy, the four friends sat in their usual spot by the window.

"OK, my young philosophers, settle down," Mr. Gebser called out with a smile. "Today we'll be discussing Jean Gebser's Concretion of Time hypothesis. It's a little advanced for an intro class, but as you may have guessed, old Jean was a relative of mine, my great grand-uncle to be precise. And this is California, so I think we can get away with it."

Ethan had heard his parents talk about Gebser's work before—they had actually wondered if Mr.

Gebser was related—so he was excited to tell them the news.

"The Concretion of Time is basically the idea that life is a process of ascending into higher and higher dimensions."

"Sounds like my dad," Sophie whispered to the other three, who all chuckled.

"So, according to this theory, life started out as tiny single-celled creatures who were only able to see or move in one direction—toward the food!"

"I can relate!" Nick grinned.

"And then after millions of years, animals and plants evolved that could move and perceive in two dimensions, backward-forward and left-right. So you could think of moss that covers a stone, or maybe even an ant that climbs over the stone. To us, these lifeforms are obviously three dimensional, but to them, the surface of the rock might as well be flat. It doesn't make any difference in their experience."

Izzy's hand shot up. "Yes, Izzy?" Mr. Gebser said.

"So, like, the rock is really 3D, but the ant only sees it as 2D?"

"It's a little more complicated than that, but that's basically right. Except we can't even say that the rock is really three dimensional, because as Einstein proved with General Relativity, time is a fourth dimension mathematically no different from the three dimensions of space. So the rock is also moving through the time dimension along with everything else, even though the rock doesn't know a dimension from an ant. And in String Theory, one of the most advanced theories in physics, there are *eleven* dimensions."

"So what about animals like a lion or a cheetah?" Izzy asked excitedly, and the class laughed.

"Many animals see three dimensions of space just like us, but even the smartest animals, like cats or dogs or apes, don't understand time in the same way we do. They don't think about their whole life, or the history of the world laid out on a timeline. They can only keep short sequences of events in their minds. So, for instance, when I get up from the dinner table, my dog, Hegel, knows it's time for his dinner and he bothers me until I give it to him. But every once in a while, I'll have lunch at the dinner table, and Hegel thinks it's time for his dinner. You should see the sad look on his face when I break the news to him!" The class laughed. "But he doesn't really understand that it's a different time of day, because he doesn't understand times of day or seasons or years or all those things related to time that we take for granted. He only knows that if I get up from the table, that means he gets his treat."

"But aren't humans animals too?" Nick asked.

"That's right, but we're special because, as far as we can tell, we're the only animals whose brains are complex enough to think about time. So we literally perceive a higher degree of freedom, as scientists say—the fourth dimension—than all of the other animals." He let that sink in for a moment as the class tried to wrap their minds around these new concepts.

Ethan raised his hand. "Yes, Ethan?" said Mr. Gebser.

"So if time is just another dimension like the three dimensions of space, why can we only move in one direction in time, but we can move in either direction in space: back and forth, side to side, or up and down?"

"That's a great question, Ethan, and the short answer is that there are a lot of theories, but no one really knows for sure." Ethan nodded. "But one possibility I find really interesting was proposed by a famous French physicist named Laurent Nottale. He discovered, through math that I don't claim to understand, that time might actually be half a dimension."

"Half a dimension?" Ethan asked. "How can you have half a dimension?"

"Well, this famous mathematician named Benoit Mandelbrot discovered something called fractals."

"I know those!" Izzy exclaimed. "They're those cool, swirly, colorful things that just keep zooming in forever."

"That's right, Izzy! That's the Mandelbrot set. But there are lots of different kinds of fractals, and Mandelbrot found that a lot of them don't have a dimension of 1, 2, or 3, but something between those, which he called fractal dimensions."

"That's so cool!" Izzy exclaimed.

"I think so too!" Mr. Gebser said, smiling. "And what I left out earlier is that the ant on the rock probably sees the world as somewhere between two and three dimensions, so the larger structure of the rock might as well be flat to the ant, but a tiny crumb would appear three dimensional to her. She only sees the smaller bumps and curves that are relevant to her scale, but the larger stuff is beyond her comprehension."

"So Mr. Gebser," Ethan asked thoughtfully, "what would it mean for time to only be half a dimension?"

"Well, that's something we don't really know, though there are a few philosophers who have speculated about it. But some people think that if we were somehow able to enhance our brains, to make them as much smarter and more complex as we are than apes, then we might be able to see the full dimension of time, rather than just half."

"Would that mean that we wouldn't just be stuck going through time in one direction, like a river?" Ethan asked. "Would we be able to time travel or something?"

"These are all great questions," Mr. Gebser said, "and philosophers aren't the only ones thinking about time. Have any of you seen the old movies *Arrival* or *Interstellar*?" About half the class nodded, including the four friends. "Well, those are visions of what it might mean to go beyond linear time, to not be stuck only going in one direction, past to future. But these are all pretty new questions, and nobody knows for sure. The very idea of time travel has really only existed for a century or so. I guess we'll just have to see what the future brings!"

CHAPTER SEVENTEEN
THE PHILOSOPHY CLUB

The bell rang, and as the class started to pack up their bags and head toward the door, Mr. Gebser came over to the four friends and said, "Hey guys, thanks for your great participation in class lately."

"No prob, Mr. G," said Izzy. "I thought philosophy was going to be boring at first, but we're all getting really into talking about it."

"Yeah," agreed Ethan, "I love hearing about all of these cool theories. I never knew time was so mysterious. It seems like it just passes and that's it, but I'm starting to realize it's a lot more complicated than that."

"I'm so glad you guys feel that way," said Mr. Gebser. "I suspected that was the case, which is why I wanted to talk to you. I'm thinking about starting a Philosophy Club that meets once a week after school to go a little deeper into all of these ideas. Would you guys be interested?"

"Definitely!" said Izzy.

"Yeah, definitely," said Ethan earnestly.

"Excellent! I'll fill out the paperwork and figure out a place to have the club."

"Thanks, Mr. Gebser," said Sophie. "It sounds like fun!"

"You're very welcome. OK, you kids have a good afternoon."

"Thanks, you too!" said Nick.

"Hey, Mr. G," said Izzy as the others made their way toward the door. "I noticed you don't have a wedding ring. Are you, like, single?"

"Um, yes, I am indeed single at the moment," Mr. Gebser responded warily.

"Oh cool," Izzy tried to sound casual, failing miserably. "It's just that my mom is really cool and pretty and she's single too, so maybe you and her could, like, I don't know, go on a date or something?"

Mr. Gebser laughed, looking relieved. "Well, I'm flattered, Izzy. If your mom has anything like your spirit, I'm sure she's an exciting woman."

"Oh, she definitely is! And she has a French accent, so . . ."

Mr. Gebser looked half amused and half intrigued. "She does sound like an interesting person. I'd love to meet her sometime."

"OK . . . cool," said Izzy with an endearing awkwardness. "See you tomorrow, Mr. G!" and she walked out the door to catch up with her friends.

CHAPTER EIGHTEEN
CONFRONTATION

The four friends walked outside and unchained their bikes, lost in thought. Then they walked their bikes down the path into the park, the girls up ahead and the boys following. "Are you thinking what I'm thinking?" Ethan said to Nick.

"If you're thinking you could go for a snack right about now, then yes."

Ethan smiled and said, "Do you think the stuff Mr. Gebser was talking about in class has anything to do with the Pleroma?"

"I don't know," Nick replied. "It does seem like quite a coincidence."

"I think we should go back into the Pleroma and ask our new friends."

"Do you think we can get back in there?" Nick looked uncertain about the prospect of venturing back into the Pleroma so soon.

"I think we have to try. Eris said they needed our help."

"OK," said Nick. "By the way, I think we need a code name in case anyone asks us what we're doing every day after school. Like a secret society."

Ethan laughed. "I kind of doubt anyone will ask."

"OK, but if they do, what should we say?" replied Nick.

Ethan thought for a moment and then said, "Why don't we tell them we're working on a project for the Philosophy Club?"

"Oh, yeah! That's great! Let's tell the girls," and they picked up the pace to catch up with Sophie and Izzy. "Hey, guys!" Nick called out as they rounded the corner by the Caves. And just as both girls turned back to look, Ethan saw the Peterson twins sitting on a big rock a little way past the path leading down to the cave entrance. They were smoking, and Milo Spencer was spray-painting some illegible red words on the side of the rock.

"Look," Ethan motioned to the others, and Izzy said, "Oh great."

"Let's just ignore them," said Sophie. Nick nodded, and they continued toward the older kids.

When they got a little closer, Connor said loudly, "Oh look, it's Tricky Nicky and his little friends," and he jumped down from the rock onto the path, followed by the others, laughing condescendingly. "What were those glasses you had at lunch?" he said menacingly. "They wouldn't happen to be your dad's new gear, would they? Let me see them."

"Yeah right!" Nick said hotly. "It's not my fault my dad's a better businessman than yours."

"What did you say?" Connor leaned forward dangerously.

"He said your dad should stop blaming everyone else for his problems!" Izzy shouted.

Connor looked furious, shouting, "Give me those glasses!" and he took a step toward Nick, followed by the others.

"Come on, let's go!" Nick called out, and he hopped on his bike back toward the way they had come, the others following. But before they even had time to get rolling, Stefan Rogan, taller than all of them by a head and beefy like a football player, stepped out of the trees onto the path.

"Stop them!" shouted Connor, and Stefan moved toward them, blocking the way.

"Oh crap!" Izzy exclaimed.

"This way!" Nick shouted. The path down to the Caves was the only way not blocked by the bullies, and it was narrow and bumpy with tree roots, so they jumped off their bikes, throwing them down between them and the high schoolers, and Nick led the others down the path toward the Caves, breaking into a run.

"Come back here!" shouted Connor, his legs momentarily tangled in the bikes. "We just want to talk to you!" And then he freed himself and led his group at a run after the younger kids.

"These guys are crazy!" shouted Izzy as they ran into the mouth of the cave, which immediately widened into a low-ceilinged cavern with openings leading off in different directions. "This way!" she shouted, and the friends all followed down a side tunnel, pulling out their phones to use as flashlights.

After only about thirty seconds of making their way through the tunnel, they came to a small cave, like a little room in the rock, with no other exits that they could see. "It's a dead end!" Nick whispered. "Let's go back and try another way!"

But then they heard Connor call out, "They're this way! I can hear them!"

"Oh no," breathed Nick. "There's nowhere to hide. What now?"

Izzy stood up straight and said, "We stand and fight."

"This feels a little too familiar," said Sophie with forced lightness.

"But this time we can't just tap out," said Nick.

"We can't give them the SPECS," Ethan said quietly, and Sophie grabbed his arm, which made his heart beat even faster than it already was.

As they heard the older kids approaching, Ethan felt a sense of rising panic very similar to what he had felt in the Orc Caverns, but this time it was real. He took a deep breath and squared his shoulders, waiting.

They saw lights coming around the bend, followed a few seconds later by Connor and the others. They stopped when their phone lights fell on the eighth graders standing up against the wall. "Well look what we have here," Connor drawled gleefully. "Some rats. Now give me those glasses!" and they moved toward the younger kids

"No!" shouted Izzy, throwing her hand in front of her, and suddenly a shaft of green light shot out of her palm, knocking the bullies to the ground.

"What did you just do?" shouted Nick.

"I don't know!" Izzy said, staring blankly at her hand.

"Let's go!" said Sophie, leading the way past the high schoolers, who were lying on the ground, still stunned from the blast. They all ran after her, out of the cave and back up the path. They jumped on their bikes and pedaled like mad until they reached Nick's house.

CHAPTER NINETEEN
CHECKING IN

They had been riding so hard that they hadn't been able to talk about what had happened in the Caves. They threw their bikes down in the driveway, still panting, and hurried through the front door. As they walked toward the steps down to the Game Room, Rob Hillman called out from the kitchen, "Kids, can you come in here for a minute?"

They stopped dead in their tracks, and Nick called out, "Hey, Dad! What are you doing home so early?" Then he turned to the others and whispered, "Don't tell him what happened." The others all nodded, Izzy looking the most reluctant, and followed Nick into the kitchen, where Rob was sitting with Ethan's parents and another man and woman at the large kitchen table. The man had pale blue eyes and a man bun, and the woman had curly brown hair and a wry expression.

"Hey, Dad, what's up?" Nick said, suddenly smiling as if he had just heard a moderately amusing joke.

"Hey, guys, have a seat. We want to check in with you about how things are going with the SPECS," Rob said cheerfully. "Ethan, have you met Sophie's dad, Mr. James, and Izzy's mom, Ms. Bergson?"

"Call me Jared, please," said the man, his blue eyes crinkling in a welcoming smile.

"And you can call me Camille," said the curly-haired woman in a pleasant French accent.

"Nice to meet you," said Ethan.

"Hey, Soph," said Jared, "your mom wanted to be here, but she had a meeting for the Caring for Our Planet benefit. Or maybe it was yoga? I can't remember." He smiled vaguely and shrugged.

They all sat at the table, and Rob poured them glasses of lemonade out of a pitcher while Christina Whitehead spoke. "How have you kids been enjoying the SPECS?" she asked.

"We love them!" Nick said. "They're really amazing," and they all nodded and murmured agreement.

"Has anything unusual happened?" she asked with a casual air, her brow slightly furrowed.

"No," said Nick, the others looking away awkwardly, "unless you'd call feeling like you're in a completely different world 'unusual!'" Nick joked, and the others laughed uneasily.

"That's good to hear," Christina said, frowning slightly, "because there was a split second at the very end of your adventure in the Orc Caverns when your brainwaves all spiked in a way that we've never seen before. It was literally just a tenth of a second or so, but are you sure nothing happened?"

They all looked at each other, and Nick said, "We were probably just freaking out because the Orcs were about to get us! Actually, I was thinking maybe that one should be PG-13. It was a little too scary for younger kids!" and the others all murmured assent.

The parents all gazed at them for a moment, and then Christina said, "OK. But be sure to tell us if anything strange happens." They all nodded and said they would.

"Alright," said Rob, "you're all staying for dinner, so you kids go have fun while we talk." The kids all got up, gave their parents hugs, and then walked toward the Game Room.

"Should we go back in the Scapes?" Ethan asked his friends as they walked down the hallway.

"I think we need a break," said Sophie, adding in a lower voice, "and we need to talk this through."

"Yeah," Izzy said, "I think we've had enough excitement for one day, and I'm tired of being indoors. It's so nice out."

Ethan looked at Nick. "Should we show them the treehouse?" he asked his friend.

"Good idea," Nick replied. "Who wants a snack?"

"I'm starving!" said Izzy, and they all laughed.

"OK," Nick said. "Ethan can take you to the treehouse. I'll go back and get us something to eat." Ethan led the girls toward the double glass doors leading out onto the patio, and Nick turned back toward the kitchen. In the hall outside the kitchen door, he heard the adults talking and paused for a moment.

"I'm still worried about the spike in their brainwaves," he heard Christina say.

"We all are," said Camille, "but I'm hearing that Jay Peterson is going to launch his new system at the VR Expo."

"That's in two weeks!" Rob exclaimed. "Is it possible that Jay has discovered the Mentalink tech too?"

"There's no way to know for sure," David replied. "He has Chris Pinker from Princeton leading his engineering team. Chris might be a jerk, and possibly even unethical sometimes, but he's a brilliant engineer. Some of his discoveries are part of what made it possible for us to develop the Mentalink technology in the first place."

"So there's a chance they might be releasing a similar tech to ours in two weeks?" Rob asked.

"Yes," Camille replied. "There's a chance, but they're being just as secretive as we are, so we won't know for sure until the Expo."

"Can we have enough SPECS ready by then?" Rob asked.

"The manufacturing isn't a problem," David replied. "We're on track to have plenty of SPECS ready for beta testing in two weeks."

Christina crossed her arms and leaned back. "I feel like the kids aren't telling us something."

"They're teenagers, Christina!" Jared laughed. "Of course there are things they're not telling us. But I trust Sophie completely. I know she would tell me if there was anything wrong with the SPECS or the Scapes. She knows how important this is."

They were all silent for a moment, and then Rob said, "Well, we can't take the chance of Jay beating us to market. He's held a grudge against me ever since we beat him with the old system. I think we have to take the risk."

"The kids will have logged more than enough hours by then to fulfill our minimum testing requirements," David chimed in.

"I think we should go for it," Jared said earnestly. "The tech is ready and the world is ready. We've done everything we can to make sure it's safe. Now it's time to put it out there and see what happens."

"What do you think, Christina?" Rob asked. "We won't do this unless the decision is unanimous."

There was a pause, and then Christina said, "I don't love it. I think it would be better if we could do more testing. But we can't let Peterson and Pinker beat us. I'm in!"

"Well, I think this calls for a celebratory adult beverage!" declared Rob.

Any thoughts of a snack forgotten, Nick turned around and jogged out the back door and across the lawn to the treehouse.

CHAPTER TWENTY
TREEHOUSE

When Nick stuck his head up through the trap door at the top of the ladder, he found his friends all sitting in bean bag chairs in the spacious treehouse, deep in conversation. "I don't know what happened," Izzy shook her head. "I just wanted to stop them, and then I felt the same thing I've been feeling practicing with the Sword of Kali in the SPECS. I was projecting my chi, but I never thought I could do it in the real world, at least not like that!" Ethan and Sophie were both listening intently.

"Hey guys," Nick said. "I have some news," and they all turned toward him. "I heard our parents talking through the kitchen door. They've decided to launch beta testing at the VR Expo in two weeks!"

"What's beta testing?" Izzy asked.

"It's where tech companies let a select group of people try out a new device before they release it to the public. I think they're going to give them to the people in the audience at the announcement. Knowing my dad, it'll be something dramatic."

"What should we do?" Izzy said. "Should we tell our parents about the Pleroma?"

"I don't think so," replied Ethan. "I don't know how to say this without sounding cheesy, so I'll just say it. I think this is destiny. The secret was shared with us, not our parents, and I think we have to respect that."

Sophie spoke up. "I feel terrible not telling my dad, but I agree. I think this is something that's bigger than all of us, and we're the ones who were chosen to see it through."

Everyone looked at Nick. "What are you looking at me for?" he blurted out. "I've always thought we shouldn't tell the parents. They'll spoil all the fun!" Everyone laughed, but there was an unmistakable nervous edge.

"OK then," Izzy said. "It's decided. We'll go back into the Pleroma tomorrow."

PART TWO

CHAPTER TWENTY-ONE
THE BEACH

The next day after school, the friends went straight down to the Game Room, sat down on the L-shaped couch, and put on their SPECS. "Which one should we do today?" asked Nick.

"How about The Beach?" said Sophie. "I want to go surfing!"

"I love surfing!" said Nick.

"I might just catch some rays and watch you guys," said Izzy, who had been quieter than usual all day.

"OK," said Ethan, "but remember, we're looking for the Cave." Everyone nodded. They all tapped on the Beach icon, and the Game Room dissolved into sparkling white sand, brilliant blue sky, and a deeper blue ocean stretching out to the horizon. They were all wearing bathing suits and sunglasses that looked exactly like the SPECS.

"This feels so nice!" Izzy declared, closing her eyes and tilting her head back to feel the full heat of the sun on her face.

Sophie grabbed a surfboard out of a stand next to them and headed toward the waves. Nick grabbed another one and turned to Ethan. "You coming?" he asked.

"No, I think I'll hang with Izzy and keep an eye out for the Cave."

"Boring!" Nick smiled, and then tucked the surfboard under his arm and ran toward the water after Sophie, shouting, "My wave, dude!"

Ethan and Izzy laughed, and then sat down next to each other on a big beach towel that was already spread near them on the sand.

They sat silently for a couple of minutes, watching Sophie and Nick catching the waves. Sophie was obviously an experienced surfer, but Nick was a bit wobbly, though he seemed to be having a great time. Then Izzy said quietly, "Nick and I got engaged when we were in preschool. He got me a ring and everything. It was plastic, but we took it very seriously." She smiled. "I'm glad we're getting close again." Then she turned to Ethan. "So Sophie's pretty great, isn't she?"

"Yeah," said Ethan earnestly. "She's awesome."

"My mom says she's 'a real throwback,' whatever that means."

Ethan laughed. "She kind of reminds me of a medieval princess." Izzy smiled at him for a second, and he felt his face flush and looked away.

"Are you blushing?" her smile got bigger.

"No!" he laughed, and they both looked back out at the waves.

"So no sign of the Cave," Izzy said, growing serious.

"Yeah, maybe we should go look for it?" Ethan suggested.

"Ok, yeah."

They got up and started walking down the beach along the water when they heard Nick yell, "Hey, guys, check it out!" They looked over and Nick was surfing standing on just one leg, the other knee raised toward his chest. Then he lost his balance and wiped out, falling off his board and going under the wave. They watched anxiously for a few seconds. Even though they knew rationally that they were in a Scape, it felt so real that it was impossible not to be worried. When Nick didn't surface, they both ran out into the waves, but Sophie got there first, paddling her board expertly through the surf with her long, thin arms. She dragged Nick up out of the water, but instead of spluttering and gasping for breath, he was laughing like a maniac.

"I can breathe underwater!" he shouted.

"Are you serious?" asked Sophie excitedly. "That's like my dream!"

"Yeah, the undertow sucked me down, and at first I thought I was drowning, but then I realized that it was just like breathing air!"

"That's so cool!" Sophie said, and dove down under the water.

"Come on, guys! You have to try this!" Nick shouted to Ethan and Izzy, who looked at each other, shrugged, and dove in after their friends.

Ethan held his breath for a moment, but then Sophie took his hand and said, her words barely audible, a bubble coming out of her mouth, "Try breathing!" Ethan let out the air he was holding in, and breathed in just a little bit, still half expecting his lungs to fill with seawater, but instead he felt them fill with air. In fact, it felt no different than it had above the waves, though he could feel the water on his skin.

"This is amazing!" he shouted, the sound muffled, and a bubble of air came out of his mouth and rose to the surface.

They swam after Nick through the crystal-clear water toward a rocky area a little farther out. When they got closer to the rocks, they saw that there was a cave in the side of the outcropping, though it wasn't glowing blue. They all looked at each other, and Nick muffle-shouted, "Let's check it out!" Nick swam into the dark cave and the others followed, but nothing happened, and the cave only went a little way back and stopped.

"Well, it was worth a try!" Ethan said, and they left the cave and swam on for another hour or so, exploring the rocks, looking at fish, and generally having a great time.

CHAPTER TWENTY-TWO
THE PETERSONS

Connor and Abigail Peterson were sitting at the dinner table with their father, Jay Peterson, who was staring dourly at his glowing tablet while the twins ate in silence. Their house was like a castle, with a lot of cold grey stone and metal, and heavy, dark wood furniture.

"Hey, Dad?" Connor said tentatively.

"Mmmm." Jay looked up from his screen. "Did you clean your room like I asked you to?"

"Yes, Dad."

"Good. And sit up straight with your shoulders back." Jay looked back at his screen.

Connor sat looking blankly at his father for a few seconds. "Dad, we saw Rob Hillman's new device."

Jay looked up sharply, his pointed nose, intense eyes, and bald head making him look like an eagle about to catch its prey. "You did?"

"Yeah," said Abigail, nervously brushing a strand of white-blond hair out of her face and smiling. "At lunch in the cafeteria, Nick Hillman and his dorky little friends were looking at some sunglasses, but they seemed a lot more interested in them than they would be if they were just normal glasses."

"So you think it was their new device? Did it look like a new technology?"

"I don't know," said Connor, "but it looked similar to your new Shades. I don't think there was room for a more powerful computer. It must just be a thinner version of the old system, like ours."

"That's good work, kids," Jay said, cracking a slight smile that didn't touch his eyes. "Well, if they've miniaturized the technology as much as we have, we'll just have to launch first at the Expo. I'm not going to let Hillman win this time." He went back to staring at his screen, and the twins took their plates to the kitchen and went to their rooms.

CHAPTER TWENTY-THREE
THE MAZE

A few days later, after school, the friends had just arrived in the Game Room at Nick's house, and they already had their SPECS on, eager to look for the Pleroma—and try another Scape.

"How about The Maze?" Ethan suggested. He and Nick had gone to a big outdoor maze up north of San Francisco once with their dads when Ethan's family was visiting the West Coast, and he remembered loving it.

"Yeah!" said Nick. "Remember the Twooz?"

"Is that what it was called?"

"Yeah, that place was awesome."

"Let's do this!" said Izzy excitedly, and they all tapped the Maze icon. The room dissolved, and they found themselves standing at the entrance to a hedge maze, the tall, deep green manicured bushes stretching off in both directions, and behind them a flat, grassy plain stretching off to some snow-capped mountains in the distance. The sky was blue and the air was pleasantly cool. Next to the entrance, there was a sign that read:

I imagined a labyrinth of labyrinths, a maze of mazes, a twisting, turning, ever-widening labyrinth that contained both past and future and somehow implied the stars.

"That's a quote from Jorge Luis Borges," said Sophie. "He's one of my dad's favorite writers."

"I love it," said Ethan thoughtfully.

"It seems weirdly relevant, doesn't it?" grinned Nick.

"Come on!" Izzy called out as she strode off into the maze.

The rest of them followed Izzy, winding through the maze for about half an hour, sometimes coming to dead ends and backtracking. It was an enjoyable way to spend some time. The weather was perfect, the company was great, and it was fun to explore the labyrinth. But they hadn't come here just for fun.

"Why can't we find the Pleroma?" Izzy said, looking frustrated.

"Yeah, it seemed like it wouldn't leave you alone before, Ethan," said Nick.

"I don't know," Ethan mused. "Maybe we're not supposed to find it yet?"

"I think that's right," said Sophie serenely. "I have a feeling that it will show itself at exactly the right time."

"OK, if you say so, Master Yoda," Nick quipped. Sophie just smiled, and they continued walking through the maze for another hour or so, finally coming to the center of the labyrinth. It was an open, grassy space, surrounded by hedges, with a large, shiny, rounded black boulder at its center. Izzy walked over to the stone, placed her hand on it, and disappeared. The others followed, and they dissolved, one by one, back into the Game Room.

CHAPTER TWENTY-FOUR
THE ROGANS

Stefan Rogan was sitting at the dinner table in his dad's condo, eating his third bowl of spaghetti carbonara. His dad, a huge former marine who now owned a cross-training gym, was currently pacing back and forth, loudly berating him after seeing the grade on his Math test. "You got a D? That's pathetic! Are you even trying?"

"Yes," Stefan said sullenly through a mouthful of spaghetti.

"Well it sure doesn't seem like it!" His dad continued. "I guess you got your mother's brains on top of her laziness." Stefan's parents had been divorced for five years, but they still fought constantly, yelling and slamming doors most of the time they had to see each other to exchange Stefan every weekend. Stefan just chewed his food and looked down. He hated his dad, but he knew that if he said anything, it would only get worse, so he sat there and took it. His mom wasn't the smartest person in the world, but at least she was nice, unlike his dad, Sergeant Jerkface. Stefan smiled to himself.

"You think that's funny?" his dad shouted.

"No, sir," Stefan mumbled.

"What's that? I can't hear you!"

"No, sir!" Stefan shouted, glaring at his father.

"Alright, I'm going for a run. I want the dishes cleaned up by the time I get back." And with that, he walked out the door, slamming it behind him.

CHAPTER TWENTY-FIVE
THE TRAIL

The friends were back in the Game Room a few days later, deciding which Scape to try next.

"How about horseback riding?" Sophie suggested. "I used to ride when I was little. It's fun."

"Sounds good to me," said Nick.

"Sure," said Ethan. "I just hope we find the Pleroma soon."

"Well, we won't find it by sitting here talking about it!" Izzy said, and she tapped the icon for The Trail. The others did the same, and they found themselves standing outside a barn. They were all wearing Western clothes, complete with cowboy hats and boots.

"Howdy, partners!" Nick mimed shooting at them with finger guns. Ethan pretended to be shot, falling down on the dusty ground, and they all laughed.

Sophie walked into the barn and the others followed. Inside, four horses stood there, saddled and ready to ride. Sophie walked up to a chestnut mare and put her hand on the horse's neck while murmuring softly. The horse nuzzled her, as if to say hello. "This is amazing," Sophie breathed. "I mean, it's one thing to recreate scenery, or even fish, but if I didn't know, I'd say that this was a real horse. The feel, the smell, the look in her eye, everything." The mare tossed her head and whinnied happily.

They each chose a horse, said hello, and led them out into the sunlight. Sophie mounted first, and they all managed to make it into their saddles, though Izzy looked like she might fall off for a minute, and then caught her balance and dragged herself up by the pommel. "I'm good!" she said confidently. Sophie led the way down the trail, moving easily with her horse, while Izzy was a little stiffer, bouncing in her saddle, but she smiled bravely and they rode on. Ethan and Nick had both ridden before on vacation with their families, so they were decent riders, but not as skilled as Sophie.

The trail meandered down through the trees, the packed red dirt winding through roots and rocks. The trees formed a canopy overhead, which made the ride pleasantly cool and shady. After a while, the trail came out of the trees by a small lake. The path was straighter here, and Sophie suggested they try a trot. They all agreed, and the horses picked up speed, Izzy bouncing along, smiling. Then Sophie picked up the pace again to a canter, and then finally a full gallop, and Izzy let out a joyful "Woo!" What she lacked in subtlety, Ethan thought, she more than made up for with enthusiasm.

After a minute or so, Sophie reined in her horse and dismounted by the lake, and the others dismounted too. "That was fun!" Izzy exclaimed.

"I'm glad you liked it," Sophie smiled.

Then Ethan saw a flash of blue out of the corner of his eye and turned, but it was only a Blue jay rising into the air. Nick caught his eye, and a silent communication passed between them. This was starting to get frustrating. When would they find the Pleroma again? Ethan hoped it wasn't too late.

CHAPTER TWENTY-SIX
THE SPENCERS

Milo Spencer sat on the couch, eating a bowl of microwave mac and cheese, watching the new movie *Nexus* on pay-per-view. It was pretty good so far. He thought it was based on a book, but he hadn't read it. He didn't read much. He mostly just watched movies and played violent games in the Scapes. He liked chaos and destruction. They soothed him.

He had the whole big house to himself as usual, except for the housekeeper, Juanita, who was really old and barely spoke English. His parents were in Europe for the next few weeks. But even when they were home, they were out almost every night at some fancy benefit and he was left to fend for himself. Whatever, he thought. A lot of kids would love to get to watch and play whatever they wanted, eat whatever they wanted, and be left alone. But Milo didn't like being alone. It made him feel insubstantial, like a ghost. The only reason he went to school every day was to see his friends, Connor and Stefan. They were kind of annoying, but they made him feel like a real person. And Abigail. He loved her, had for years, but he barely spoke to her even though they were together all the time. She was a princess and he was just some creepy kid who lived alone in an empty house, like some dark sorcerer hiding in his cave.

He took another bite of mac and cheese and washed it down with soda. He was sick of mac and cheese. And soda. Maybe he would text Connor and Stefan and see if they wanted to meet up and go steal some gum or something from the store.

CHAPTER TWENTY-SEVEN
HAUNTED HOUSE

"Alright, guys," Nick said. "Which Scape should we try next?"

"How about Haunted House?" grinned Izzy.

"Yeah!" said Sophie enthusiastically.

"OK, sure," Ethan agreed. He didn't really like haunted houses, but he didn't want the girls to think he was scared. And they might as well check all of the Scapes for the Pleroma.

They all tapped on the icon, and they found themselves standing on the porch of a decrepit old mansion, the sky swirling with dark, menacing clouds, and wind howling through barren trees, like skeletal hands reaching up from the ground. "Creepy!" said Izzy excitedly.

"We love haunted houses," Sophie told Ethan with a grin.

"Oh . . . yeah," Ethan said with a forced smile.

"Well, we're not going to find the Pleroma standing here!" said Nick, and he led the way into the spooky old house.

Inside, there was a strong musty smell, and there were lit candelabras covered with spider webs. As they made their way into the long hallway leading deeper into the house, the ancient floorboards creaked with every step, and they could still hear the wind whistling outside. Halfway down the hall, a strong draft of wind suddenly blew out all the candles and they found themselves in near darkness. Ethan felt Sophie's hand grab his and squeeze, and his stomach fluttered, not only from fear. "I thought you liked haunted houses!" Ethan whispered.

"I do!" Sophie whispered breathlessly. "Creeps!"

They walked on for a moment, and then they heard a moan coming from upstairs. "Let's go!" Izzy said, and they went through an open door at the end of the hallway. The room was dark, and they couldn't tell how large it was. Ethan and Sophie were last into the room and, suddenly, the door slammed shut behind them and hundreds of candles sprang to life, revealing a large ballroom with a huge crystal chandelier at the center. A piano started playing some creepy classical music, though there was no one playing. Then a procession of ghostly lords and ladies emerged from the walls, their ghoulish, twisted faces as transparent as their gowns and top hats. "Eek!" Izzy let out a squeal that sounded more thrilled than frightened, and she grabbed Nick's arm, who just looked amused, though he flinched when a ghostly couple started waltzing in their direction.

"Let's keep going!" Ethan whispered. "We have to find the Cave." He led the way across the room, carefully avoiding colliding with the dancers, who seemed oblivious to their presence, and into a large kitchen. Everything was quiet for a moment, and they just stood there listening. Then the pots and pans hanging from metal hooks started rattling fiercely, and one flew toward Nick's head, who ducked it just in time.

"This way!" Izzy shouted, and they ran through another door as a knife embedded itself in the wall where they had just been standing. Ethan quickly slammed the door shut, and they heard metal clanging against the wood as they made their way down the hall to a rickety-looking staircase leading upstairs. "Should we go up?" Izzy asked, grinning.

"We could always tap out," Nick said, trying to act blithe, but betrayed by his ragged breathing.

"No way!" said Izzy. "I want to see what's up there!"

"And we have to keep looking for the Pleroma," Ethan added grimly, and Nick nodded.

"Come on, guys," Sophie laughed. "This is supposed to be fun!" And she led the way up the stairs, pulling Ethan by the hand.

At the top of the stairs was another long hallway, lit with candelabras, and they made their way toward a door at the far end. When they reached the door, it creaked open without any of them touching it. They all looked at each other, and Izzy, still grinning, led the way into the shadowy room. There was a large four-poster bed hung with moth-eaten white curtains. And there appeared to be someone lying in the bed, though it was hard to tell in the dim light. Ethan took a step closer to get a better look, and the figure sat up like a shot, a zombie wearing a tattered night dress and cap. It looked at them with bulging eyes and let out a terrifying scream! They stumbled out of the room, the scream still echoing, and ran down the hallway, down the stairs, and out the back door of the house into a garden of decaying plants. They were all panting and laughing hysterically.

"Alright, that's it," Nick said. "I think we're done here."

"OK, fine." Izzy replied. "But that was fun!"

"Uh, yeah," said Nick. "Fun." He tapped his temple where the button would be on his SPECS and disappeared, and they all did the same, reappearing in the Game Room. Ethan was glad to be done with that Scape.

"So where is the Cave?" Izzy said.

"I don't know," said Ethan. "I'm starting to wonder if we'll ever be able to get back in. I mean, I believed Eris when she said we'd see her soon, but why aren't they letting us back in?"

"Yeah," said Nick, "I thought they needed our help?"

Sophie said quietly, "One thing I've learned meditating with the pendant is that things tend to happen at exactly the right time. I don't know why they're making us wait, but I have a feeling we'll be back in the Pleroma when we're needed."

"I hope you're right," said Ethan.

CHAPTER TWENTY-EIGHT
SURPRISE

It was now only two days until the Expo, and they still hadn't found the Cave. They all went back to Nick's house after school, as usual. When they walked into the kitchen, Rob, Christina, and David were sitting around the kitchen table waiting for them.

"Hey, kids," Rob said jovially. "Come have a seat. We want to check in one more time before the launch on Saturday."

They all sat down, and Rob looked at Christina, who said, "I think you guys know by now what I'm going to ask. Has anything unusual happened?"

They all shook their heads. "No, Mom," Ethan said, relieved that he didn't have to lie. "We've just been enjoying the Scapes."

"Yeah," said Izzy, "the boys loved the Haunted House." She smiled.

"Oh, really?" said Christina. "I thought you didn't like haunted houses, Ethan?"

"It was OK," Ethan mumbled, glancing over at Sophie.

"Your brainwaves have been completely normal," Christina continued, "and the spike only happened that once, so unless there's anything else you guys want to tell us, I think we're good to go." She looked intently into all of their faces in turn, and they all shook their heads.

"OK, then!" Rob said. "So which Scapes are your favorites?"

"I loved The Beach!" said Sophie. "Oh, and the Trail!"

"My favorites were probably The Slopes and The Maze," said Ethan.

"Space Battle!" declared Nick, and everyone laughed.

"I actually think my favorite was the Orc Caverns," said Izzy, "even though we didn't finish the adventure." She looked at her friends. "But the Haunted House was pretty great too!" And they all laughed again.

"Great," said Rob. "That's a nice variety. We're proud of all of the Scapes. Your dad's team did a fantastic job, Sophie." Sophie looked pleased, and Rob continued, "We've just finished testing one more Scape that we're going to let everyone in the audience try at the launch."

"What is it?" asked Nick.

"It's a surprise," Rob responded, smiling. "I think you'll love it."

CHAPTER TWENTY-NINE
BLUE

Later that evening, Blue McKenna was loading the dishwasher and listening to music. Rob walked into the kitchen and said, "Thanks so much, Blue. You're too good to us."

"I don't mind at all, Rob," she said in her Irish accent.

"What are you listening to?"

"It's the new album from Ásgeir."

"What's that?"

"He's a singer from Iceland. His first album was the biggest selling debut in the country's history. They say ten percent of Icelanders own a copy."

He listened for another few seconds. "I love it! I'm lucky to have a hip young lady like you around to keep me up to date on all the new music."

"I'm not that young anymore," she smiled. "And you're not that old!"

"Thanks for saying that, Blue." Rob smiled wistfully. "You've been such a great help since the divorce. I don't have to tell you how busy I am, but you've given Nicky such a sense of stability, and he just adores you. You make this place feel like a home. I hope you never leave us."

"I'm happy right where I am." Blue smiled up at Rob, their eyes meeting for a long moment.

"Well, I'm going to go try to catch up on my mountain of emails," he said.

"Good luck with that!" They both laughed.

After Rob left the room, Blue stared abstractedly out the window over the sink, a plate forgotten in her rubber-gloved hand. She was thirty-four now, and she had been with the Hillmans since she had graduated from San Francisco State. Thirteen years. She had originally thought that she would do something in the music business, maybe manage bands. But the Hillmans had been wonderful to work for. Rob and Nicole, Nick's mother, had always been kind to her, paid her extremely well, and gave her plenty of time off. She had come to love Nick as she watched him grow, really raised him as much as his parents. And she had fallen in love with Rob. She wasn't sure exactly when it had happened. It had kind of snuck up on her. She had never said anything to him about it, and he had been nothing but a perfect gentleman, even after the divorce. But in the last year or so, their gazes into one another's eyes had been getting longer and more meaningful.

She knew she was being stupid. He was a handsome billionaire and she was a nanny turned housekeeper. But she couldn't help it. She loved him, and she had no idea what to do about it. She didn't want to upset the perfect balance the three of them had established. She couldn't say anything to him.

But she felt sure that he loved her too. He hadn't been on a date since the divorce even though he was considered one of the most eligible bachelors in the world. Maybe she was just fooling herself. But she saw the way he looked at her. It couldn't go on like this. Something had to give.

She looked down and realized she was still holding the dirty plate, and put it in the dishwasher. She put in the soap, started it up, and looked around. Everything was clean and tidy in the big, gorgeous house she had spent some of the best years of her life in. She grabbed her bag from off a kitchen stool and walked toward the front door. On the way, she passed by Rob's office and called out, "Good night."

He looked up and smiled warmly. "Good night, Blue. See you tomorrow." She walked out the door, got in her car, and headed out to see some bands with a friend.

CHAPTER THIRTY
EXPO

On the morning of the Virtual Reality Expo, the four friends were walking through the rows and rows of booths set up by hundreds of tech companies. There were booths displaying goggles, gloves, and full-body suits in various shapes and colors, cameras and microphones for recording live experiences, and holographic videos of games and apps for the various devices hovering in the air. People throughout the hall were testing out the devices in roped-off areas, interacting with worlds only they could see in their goggles. Ethan thought they looked kind of silly. He patted his jacket pocket where he had his SPECS safely hidden away in their case. "The SPECS are going to blow all of this away," he said quietly to his friends.

"Yeah," said Nick. "My dad keeps talking about how it's going to completely change the industry, and everyone is going to have to scramble to catch up."

Izzy mused, "It's a little sad that all of these people are putting so much time and energy . . ."

"And money," Nick chimed in.

"And money," Izzy added, "into stuff that's going to be obsolete in a few hours."

"I know," said Nick, "but that's the name of the game. As my dad says: 'You can't stop the progress train, so you might as well get on board.'"

"Your dad says that?" asked Izzy, laughing.

"Yeah," Nick said. "He's kind of a nerd. But hey, this is Silicon Valley, where nerds rule. And my dad is King of the Nerds!"

"Alright, Nerd Prince," Izzy grinned.

"Hey, I thought the ridiculous nicknames were my thing!" Nick grinned back.

"Nerd Prince?" said Connor Peterson's voice, dripping with condescension. And there were Connor, Abigail, Stefan, and Milo standing by a booth, trying on some gloves.

"So you think you're nerds?" asked Abigail with an expression somewhere between concerned and mocking.

Milo glared at them darkly through his stringy black hair. "What did you do to us in that cave, anyway? Was that a flash grenade?"

"I don't know what you're talking about," Izzy said defensively. "Just leave us alone."

"Why don't you make us," said Stefan, looming threateningly.

"Never mind, Stef." Connor put his hand on his friend's shoulder, and Stefan looked at him, his eyes softening. "Their dad's about to get crushed anyway," said Connor. "Our dad's launch is first, and there's no way your dad will beat him this time."

"We'll see about that," said Nick. "Let's get out of here," and the four friends walked away quickly, feeling the eyes of the four older kids on their backs.

CHAPTER THIRTY-ONE
THE SHADES

About an hour later, the friends were sitting in the back row of the auditorium when Jay Peterson and another man with curly brown hair walked onto the stage. "Hello, everyone! I'm Jay Peterson, and this is my Head of Engineering, Chris Pinker!" The audience clapped politely. "Today, we are making the biggest announcement in Virtual Reality since the release of the Oculus Rift back in 2012!" He paused for effect while the audience murmured. "We present . . . The Shades!" And on the large screen behind Peterson and Pinker, a picture of what looked like

156

wrap-around mirror sunglasses appeared. The audience clapped, and someone let out a "Woo!" Ethan looked over and saw that it had been Stefan Rogan, down closer to the stage.

"Oof, those are trosh," whispered Izzy, and Sophie nodded agreement.

"What does 'trosh' mean?" whispered Ethan to Sophie.

"You know, short for 'atrocious,'" she replied. Ethan laughed.

When the clapping died down, Peterson continued. "These are the slimmest, most compact, most undetectable monitors that have ever existed!" The audience clapped, while Peterson pulled a pair out of his jacket pocket and put them on. "They look and feel exactly like regular sunglasses, but with better power and resolution than the old, clunky headsets and goggles! Welcome to the revolution!" More clapping, though the audience wasn't quite as enthusiastic as Peterson seemed to think they were.

"So does this mean that they don't have the Mentalink technology?" Izzy asked.

"It doesn't sound like it," said Nick.

"Thank goodness," said Sophie. "I almost feel sorry for the guy, except that he's such a jerk."

"Yeah, same with his kids," Nick replied.

"Those really are ugly glasses," Ethan remarked. "They remind me of that guy who took us deep-sea fishing that one time," Ethan whispered to Nick.

"You mean the guy with the big beer belly and the horrible sunburn?" Nick laughed.

"Yeah," Ethan smiled. "He was a nice guy, but not exactly a fashion icon."

CHAPTER THIRTY-TWO
LAUNCH

There was a thirty-minute break before The SPECS launch when everyone was asked to leave the auditorium for cleaning. The friends wandered through the booths, wondering excitedly about what the new Scape would be and how people would respond to the new technology. After about twenty minutes, the auditorium reopened and they found some seats down near the front. Finally, the lights dimmed again, and Rob Hillman and Christina and David Whitehead walked onto the stage. The SPECS logo filled the huge screen behind them.

Rob, with a showman's flair, jumped right in: "Have you ever wanted to fly? Our new device, based on a completely new technology we call Mentalink, doesn't just simulate the sights and sounds of flying like the older VR systems. You will actually *feel* like you're flying. But don't take my word for it. Look under your seats!" Everyone in the auditorium leaned down and pulled out white cases that had apparently been taped under the seats during the break. "We are excited to present: SPECS!" Everyone was pulling the devices out of their cases and examining them. "SPECS stands for Sensory Perception Emulation Control Systems, and we promise, they're like nothing you've ever experienced!"

The people in the packed, one-thousand-seat auditorium, mostly tech journalists and people from other companies, put the SPECS on, murmuring excitedly. The friends pulled out their own SPECS, put them on, and tapped the buttons at their temples. The auditorium immediately dissolved, and they found themselves standing in a large field under a blue sky with fluffy white clouds. People were popping into existence all around them, looking stunned and awed by the reality of the experience, some of them letting out cries of delight. From the center of the field, Rob, Christina, and David rose up into the air above the watching crowd, who let out a collective "Aaaahhh!" Rob called out, his arms spread wide, "All you have do is jump!" And with that, people started launching themselves into the air, first just a few, and then hundreds, many of them shouting with elation.

"Come on!" Nick called out, and they all jumped, but instead of the usual feeling of gravity pulling them back down to earth, they just kept rising. It was an unbelievably thrilling feeling, the ancient dream to fly through the air like a bird—or a superhero—finally realized! As they rose up into the air, they saw Rick Taylor, the balding CEO of one of the biggest computer companies in the world, doing backflips and laughing hysterically. It was impossible not to smile watching him vault through the air.

They continued rising, Ethan swooping back and forth with a mere thought, Nick leading the way higher and higher, looking down at the ecstatic crowd. Then suddenly they were inside of a cloud, unable to see more than a foot in front of them, their clothes and skin damp. And then they burst through the top of the cloud and the sun shone brilliantly off a billowing white landscape spread out below them, like a movie version of heaven or Mount Olympus. They all laughed and shouted with the sheer splendor of it, the feeling of complete freedom and weightlessness finally satisfying some primal yearning deep in their chests. They spun around each other in somersaults, reveling in the experience.

Then Ethan saw a blue flash out of the corner of his eye. He looked over, and there was the Cave in the side of a hill made of clouds. "There it is!" he shouted to his friends over the rushing wind. "The Cave!"

They all turned toward it, and Izzy shouted, "Should we go in?"

Ethan shouted back, "This might be our last chance!" They all shouted agreement and flew straight into the flickering blue portal that they had been searching for these last few weeks.

Unnoticed by the four friends, Connor, Abigail, Milo, and Stefan had been sitting at the back of the auditorium, and they had appeared in the Scape near the edge of the crowd, watching as Sophie, Izzy, Nick, and Ethan rose into the air. "Come on, let's try it," Stefan said after most of the crowd was already airborne. He jumped into the air, whooping with glee, followed by Abigail and Milo, and then, grudgingly, Connor, his arms crossed, a sour look on his face.

As they shot up into the air, Connor shouted, "So what? It's just flying. I don't think it's that great!"

"I think it's amazing!" shouted Stefan.

"Yeah, Conn, I hate to say it," shouted Abigail to her twin, "but this is pretty incredible. Dad's going to be pissed!"

Milo, smiling crookedly as if he wasn't used to making the expression, let out a wordless cry, and followed Abigail. After a minute or two, they burst out of the top of the clouds. Stefan shouted, "Look!" and pointed to the younger kids diving into a glowing blue hole in the side of a cloud.

"Where are they going?" shouted Abigail.

"I don't know!" yelled Connor. "Let's follow them!" and they all flew toward the flickering opening. They hesitated for a moment a few feet away, looking at each other, and then Connor dove in, the others following.

CHAPTER THIRTY-THREE
RETURN TO THE PLEROMA

For the second time, Ethan found himself falling through blackness, twisting, slipping sideways through a crack at the edge of his vision. And then he was standing on the platform in the vast space, surrounded by staircases that didn't make sense, feeling as if he was looking through a fish-eye lens.

There was a blinding white flash, which made him close his eyes. When he opened them, there floated Eris, her white hair and robes rippling in an unfelt wind, her eyes like bottomless chasms in her ageless face. He looked down, and then dropped to one knee as he had before. It seemed like the right thing to do.

"Hello, Ethan." Eris' melodious voice seemed to come from everywhere. "Welcome back to the Pleroma. It is good to see you again."

"Thanks . . . It's good to see you too." Ethan wondered if he should call her by a title. Ma'am? Your Majesty? What are you supposed to call a being made of light from another world? Deciding to just not call her anything, he continued. "We've been looking for the Cave—the Gateway—for weeks. Why haven't we been able to find it until now?"

"You have returned to us at just the right time, Ethan. All is as it should be."

"But didn't you say you needed our help? Isn't that kind of urgent?"

"Yes, Ethan. You will help us very soon. But first, you have questions. Ask them."

"OK." Ethan racked his brain, trying to bring back all of the questions that had been burning in him these last few weeks, but they seemed to have drained out of his head. Then it occurred to him. "What is the Pleroma? Where are we?"

"This is a larger manifold, Ethan, a higher degree of freedom."

"Like a higher dimension?"

"Yes, Ethan. The domain you and your people inhabit has three dimensions of space and one dimension of time. But your physicists and philosophers are only beginning to understand what your shamans and sages have intuitively understood for many millennia. What you call 'time' is simply another dimension, like space. But in your domain, you can only see a part of that dimension. Here, you can see the whole thing, though you are like a newborn, seeing the world for the first time."

"So Gebser's and Nottale's ideas about time are right? Time is a fractal dimension?"

"Yes, Ethan. That is one way to describe it."

"But I still don't understand exactly what that means. How can time be only a part of a dimension?"

"Do not worry, Ethan. You have already come far closer to understanding the Pleroma than most of your kind. While those in your domain can move at will in the three dimensions of space, they have no freedom to move in time. Rather, they are carried along like a raft on a river, and they cannot see into the future or past, other than in memory or foresight. But here, we see through time just like you can look backward and forward or left and right. It is simply another direction in which to look."

"So you can time travel?"

"In a way, but it is not like in most of your books or films, where you step into a phone booth and step out in the age of the dinosaurs or Napoleon. We move through time just like you, in one direction, because the dimension of time is being pulled onward by a force similar to gravity, which your mathematicians call a Strange Attractor."

"I'm sorry, I don't understand."

"Do not worry, Ethan. As I said, you are like a newborn baby in this domain. You cannot expect to be able to make sense of it until you have spent more time here."

"But I want to understand!"

"Very well, I will tell you one thing more, and then it will be time for you to help us."

"How will we help you?"

"All will become clear, Ethan. But first, I will say that we were once like you, unable to see through the time dimension. Then we discovered the Gateway, and we transformed into something new, as different from what we were before as you are from your primate ancestors."

"So you evolved?"

"Yes, Ethan, in a manner of speaking. We believe that everything in the universe constantly evolves. But as I said, although we can see through time, we move through it like you, as if pulled by the force of gravity, falling down a very deep well."

"I think I understand," said Ethan. "So you're pulled through time just like us by this Strange Attractor, but you can see what happens in the future and the past?"

"That is right, Ethan," Eris responded, smiling benignly, "but there are others who are to us as we are to you. They have found a way to resist the pull of the Strange Attractor, to move through the fourth dimension at will. We will become like them someday, but not yet."

Suddenly, the Pleroma started to shake, and the staircases, stable until now in their bizarre fashion, started to slide and rotate in ways that made Ethan's stomach churn. Eris closed her eyes for a moment, and when she opened them, she looked gravely serious. "Now it is time for you to help us, Ethan."

"What can I do?" he pleaded, the space becoming more and more chaotic by the moment.

"Four others of your kind have followed you and your friends into the Pleroma, Ethan. Their intentions are not as pure."

"Others?" Ethan asked, confused.

"They are young ones, a little older than you, almost too old to find the Pleroma at all."

"Oh no!" Ethan cried. "It must be Milo, Stefan, and the Peterson Twins!"

"You must face them, Ethan," Eris said solemnly. "You and your friends must each face your counterpart and decide for your world what the

Pleroma will be for you. Be steadfast. I will see you soon." And with a flash she was gone, but the Pleroma continued to writhe and twist in increasingly bizarre convolutions.

CHAPTER THIRTY-FOUR
BATTLE FOR THE PLEROMA

As if coming around an impossible curve, Ethan could see Nick standing at the top of a mountain. A lightning storm raged around him, his hair standing up in a comical way. Nick raised his hand in greeting, and Ethan did the same, smiling. It seemed somehow wrong to shout here, and he wasn't sure Nick would be able to hear him anyway. The normal rules of space and time didn't seem to apply. Then, coming around another impossible curve to his left, Ethan saw Sophie swimming underwater, her dark red hair floating in the turbulent depths. She smiled at him, and he smiled back. She looked like a beautiful mermaid. Then again, to his right, he saw Izzy standing at the mouth of a volcano. Lava spurted violently all around the large, flat boulder on which she was standing. She raised her fist in salute to Ethan, a proud warrior preparing for battle. Ethan solemnly returned the gesture.

A blue Gateway suddenly opened above another platform in Ethan's staircase world, though Ethan found it impossible to estimate the distance. Out dropped Milo Spencer, landing lightly and looking around dazed. Then he saw Ethan, and scowled. "You," he said. "Where are we?"

"This place is called the Pleroma," Ethan replied. "Why did you follow us?"

"Well," Milo considered, "Connor hates you guys because of your parents. I don't care about that. I just don't like you."

"Why? What did I ever do to you?"

"You were born. And you're just so disgustingly sweet and innocent. I bet your parents still tuck you in at night."

Ethan didn't know what to say to that. His parents *did* still tuck him in. Was that a bad thing? "So what's your point?" Ethan shouted. "What do you want?"

"I want chaos!" And with that, black tendrils of smoke emerged from Milo's fingertips. He looked down at them quizzically, and then smiled. "Whatever this place is, I think I like it!" And he flung his hands toward Ethan, the black tendrils shooting like writhing snakes at the younger boy. Ethan, without thinking, put up his hands, palms forward. Shifting prisms made of white light blossomed out of them, expanding rapidly to meet the black tendrils, order rising to meet strife. And then they clashed. The tendrils turned aside at the angular surfaces of the prismatic light, worming their way between the cracks in the structures. Ethan willed the prisms to transform in complex ways, redirecting the tendrils away from him. He turned them back again and again with a placid mathematical harmony. But the tendrils snaked around the edges of each defensive movement until the dark strands were hopelessly intertwined with the light prisms. The two boys were locked in a fierce duel of wills, neither moving. Their whole bodies were taut with the strain of trying to push the other back, to gain some advantage.

And in the midst of this stalemate between order and chaos, Ethan could somehow see Izzy and Stefan Rogan. They were standing on the large, flat boulder, lava flowing all around them, engaged in a fierce battle. Stefan was shooting tongues of flame from his hands, and Izzy met them with thick shafts of green light. They were almost like leafy vines growing out of her palms. The green shafts withered in the onslaught of the flames, but surged on, growing as fast as the fire could singe them. They too were locked in a stalemate, the forces of creation and destruction, neither able to gain the upper hand.

Ethan could see Nick and Connor Peterson standing at the peak of the stormy, windswept mountain. Blue electricity crackled and coursed between them. Ethan could somehow tell that each of the boys was trying to bend the other's mind to his own. They were creating competing illusions, trying to trick the other into submitting. The electricity surged back and forth, but neither boy seemed able to get the advantage.

And Ethan could See Sophie and Abigail Peterson floating underwater, gazing into one another's eyes. Both of the girls were smiling weirdly in some subtle standoff Ethan didn't quite understand. A roiling darkness surrounded Abigail, seeking to encroach on a calm brightness surrounding Sophie. The two shades seemed to ebb and flow like barely discernible moods borne back and forth on the tide, neither able to vanquish the other.

Ethan continued to face off against Milo's onslaught of chaos. He transformed the prisms in more and more complex patterns, but he was unable to push out Milo's increasingly entangled tendrils. And little by little, he realized that he could sense his friends' thoughts. It wasn't so much like listening to a radio, but like seeing and feeling the images in their heads. And he understood that they could sense him too.

Ethan could feel Izzy's fierce determination, but also her fear that she couldn't compete with the bigger, stronger boy, that he was just too powerful. Pushing against the back of her mind, echoing the devouring flames pushing against her green light, were the voices of everyone who had ever told her that girls aren't as tough as boys. She felt every TV show and movie she had ever seen that had shown a woman taking second place to a man, giving up her dreams and desires so that he could have his, so he could talk while she listened. She felt that it was too much, that no matter how much energy she put into the green shafts, Stefan's angry fire devoured them. With this thought, she fell to her knees. She didn't know how much longer she could resist his fury.

And then Ethan sensed Nick fantasizing about his parents getting back together. He felt a deep regret and sadness drawn out by Connor, leading Nick's mind down a dark path. Nick resisted, struggling to find the place in Connor's mind that would lead him away from this darkness, this craving for revenge and dominance. He tried with all his might to instill the belief in Connor that the two boys were at peace, even friends. But Nick started to feel despair well up in him, a deep sadness he had repressed and avoided feeling. The break-up of his family was almost too much to bear, and he felt the seductive pull of the image of his parents holding hands in the sunlight, smiling and laughing. He didn't know how much longer he could resist succumbing to its lure.

And then Ethan's mind turned to Sophie, facing the smiling Abigail, though with that condescending tightness around her eyes. Ethan realized that Abigail reminded Sophie strongly of her mother: so beautiful, so thin, so stylish, so *perfect*. Sophie felt like she could never live up to her mother's expectations. She couldn't ignore the passive-aggressive comments, always delivered with a smile. They ate away at the peaceful serenity inside of her that she felt called to bring into the light, to share with others. It was a like a worm in a perfect-looking apple, with Abigail reaching in and twisting, smiling, always smiling.

As Ethan sensed his friends beginning to falter in the onslaught from the older kids, he felt his own defenses starting to weaken. Milo's dark tendrils began to advance slowly, slipping into the cracks of Ethan's transforming prisms. The tendrils were relentless. Milo's eyes mocked the order that Ethan clung to, the structure of light that seemed to be slipping from his grasp.

Ethan closed his eyes, searching through the vast amount of knowledge he had been given by *The Book of Eris*. He was desperately looking for some concept, some theory that could help him to create an airtight wall of order against Milo's insidious chaos. He wanted to destroy the darkness and replace it with light. But the more he struggled and pushed, the more deeply the shadowy tendrils became intertwined with his prisms. And a panic began to rise in him, a deep fear that the chaos would overwhelm him, drown him in its dark, swirling embrace.

And then it came to him, all at once, a thousand images of men and women, in furs and robes and suits, around campfires and in temples and lecture halls. Suddenly he understood what many shamans and sages and philosophers had understood before. Order can never defeat chaos. As soon as you think you've finally stamped it out, it will rise again somewhere else, twice as strong. Order without chaos is sterile, dead. Ethan realized, a thousand voices chanting in his head in a thousand different languages, that to overcome the chaos, he must surrender to it. The chaos, he realized, was not only in Milo, but also in him. Order could not exist without chaos, and chaos could not exist without order.

Then he saw something buried deep inside Milo, a seed of light. Ethan stopped resisting, opening himself to the dark tendrils. The prisms of light relaxed into an ordered lattice with labyrinthine pathways through which the newly liberated tendrils shot. They filled the empty spaces, moving toward Ethan. Then, out of Ethan's fingertips blossomed new black tendrils, coursing through the prismatic brilliance. They merged with the tendrils from Milo's fingers that he had been resisting all this time. And to Milo's great astonishment, out of his palms emerged prisms of light. They wrapped themselves around the dark strands, containing them in a loving embrace. Finally, between Ethan and Milo was an enormously complex structure of intertwined light and darkness, a perfect balance of chaos and order. And Ethan understood that inside his parents' good boy, their perfect child, was also a creative chaos that yearned to be let loose, to find the freedom to go beyond his well-ordered world. And Milo felt, finally, his destructive chaos being contained, held by the order and structure his parents' absence had denied him.

The two boys stood there, looking at one another. They were both exhausted and exhilarated, both feeling transformed. And they began to see one another through the other's eyes. Milo was no longer merely a sinister, cruel villain, but a lonely, sad fourteen-year-old boy craving belonging and purpose. And Ethan was no longer merely a naïve, sheltered puppet of his parents' expectations, but a confused thirteen-year-old boy craving experience, reveling in the freedom of recognizing his own shadow in addition to the light. In embracing Milo, Ethan had conquered the destructive darkness by finding that shadow in himself and reconciling with it. And now the two boys would be bonded forever.

Nodding to Milo in silent accord, Ethan stretched his new sense out and could feel Izzy, reinvigorated by Ethan's act. She rose to her feet and let out a fierce battle cry, her green force pushing back Stefan's fire until they were in equilibrium. And then, unexpectedly, in the place where the orange fire and green light met, a ball of concentrated white light began to grow. And instead of pushing against one another, Izzy and Stefan both began to send their energy into the glowing orb, which grew bigger and brighter. Suddenly, rather than being at odds, Izzy and Stefan found themselves working together to create this force between them. And as it grew, they both started laughing, and then shouting in joyful triumph. They shouted not because one had defeated the other, but because they had both overcome themselves to become part of something greater, the beginning of something completely new.

Ethan, smiling with Izzy and Stefan, shifted his attention to Nick. He was entranced by the image of his parents laughing, holding hands. But the surge of energy from Milo and Ethan's integration of chaos and order, and from Stefan and Izzy's integration of creation and destruction, shocked Nick out of his trance. As if waking from a dream, he could now see that it was healthy to feel sad about his parents splitting up, that it was their choice and that he had to trust that it was the best thing for all of them. Nick allowed the sadness to wash over him, and it swept away the last vestiges of the illusion, the lie that Connor had plucked from his mind.

And then Nick turned his attention to his nemesis. He stepped past the boundary of his consciousness into Connor's. He stepped past the condescending sneer to find a sad, angry boy whose mother had died when he was young, and who craved his father's approval but mostly received criticism. The boy tried, over and over, to live up to his father's expectations, but his hopes were dashed again and again. Connor looked down for a moment, ashamed that his secret had been revealed. And then he looked straight into Nick's eyes. Both boys recognized the other's pain behind their trickster masks, Nick's goofy performer and Connor's mocking critic. And as they looked into one another's eyes, the masks began to transform. Their fixed roles became more fluid, flickering frantically from one role to the next. And after a while, the masks began to synchronize, to mirror one another, transforming at a less frantic pace. And then, as one, the two boys realized that the masks were their faces. They understood that, by sharing their honest pain, they had made their trickster masks identical with their true selves, the boys behind the masks. Suddenly none of their previous conflict mattered. This was an experience that very few people had ever gone through, and it created an unbreakable bond between them. They both smiled, eyes twinkling mischievously at their shared secret.

Ethan turned his attention to Sophie. Her light shrank before the onslaught of darkness projected by Abigail, whose face looked remarkably like Sophie's mother, smiling her perfect, condescending smile. But then Sophie felt the force of reconciliation surging from Ethan and Milo to Izzy and Stefan to Nick and Connor and into her. She closed her eyes for a moment. And when she opened them, Sophie realized that behind the cruelly shining beacon of perfection that made her feel small, Abigail was hollow, yearning for connection. Like her twin, Abigail had also lost her mother at a young age, lost her model of what it meant to be a woman. And though her father was less critical of her than her brother, his affection was just as scarce. And so she turned to magazines and movies and her phone, learning the secrets of beauty and style and feminine grace as a way to hide her deep sorrow and loneliness.

As Sophie gazed at Abigail, she began to feel compassion, even love for this girl who had made her feel so flawed. Sensing this shift, the contempt drained out of Abigail's eyes, and they became soft, welling with tears. Sophie floated through the water toward her, and embraced the older girl. Abigail had been shining a harsh light on Sophie's flaws to cover her own. But now that Abigail's pain had been revealed and accepted by Sophie, there was nothing left to hide. And as they hugged, they laughed, tears streaming out of their eyes and mingling with the water.

The lattice of chaos and order between Ethan and Milo dissolved, as did the ball of light between Izzy and Stefan, though they could still feel its echo. The electricity around Nick and Connor settled down to a mild crackling. And the shades of dark and light around Sophie and Abigail mingled to form a dappled pattern, like light gently shining through leaves onto a forest floor.

There was a bright flash, and they all stood together on an endless plain under a twilight sky, eight kids who had just experienced something unprecedented. And without speaking, they all looked at one another. The profound ordeal they had shared wiped away all of their previous resentments like a fading dream.

And then Ethan saw, off at the horizon, a figure of light appear, rushing toward them at great speed.

"Look!" Izzy called out, and there were three other figures rushing from each of the other three cardinal directions, converging on the group. And then the beings were there, hovering before them, encircling them in a benevolent embrace: Prometheus, Vishnu, Kali, and Eris, radiating power and mystery.

CHAPTER THIRTY-FIVE
THE EIGHT

The eight kids stood there, overwhelmed by the struggle they'd just gone through together, and by the appearance of these powerful beings encircling them. The beings radiated light, their clothes and hair flowing, but their faces impassive. After a moment, Ethan went down on one knee, grabbing Milo's sleeve and pulling him down too. The others followed, each pair facing a different being, the older kids looking to the younger ones for guidance in this extraordinary experience.

Eris' melodious voice filled the air, as if they were in a small room, though the plain stretched off in all directions to the horizon. "You have done well, all of you. We are grateful."

Kali, her skin blue, her four arms holding various weapons, and a halo of fire blazing around her fierce head, spoke in a penetrating voice. "It was a great battle, one that will be remembered by your people for a very long time," and she nodded respectfully to Izzy and Stefan kneeling before her.

"You have chosen the way of compassion and unification rather than hatred and division," said the equally blue-skinned and four-armed Vishnu, hovering, legs crossed in a lotus posture, his face smiling serenely down at Sophie and Abigail.

"This is the right path," said Prometheus, a muscular, bearded man in a toga. "You have chosen the way of insight and discovery over the path of disruption and the breaking apart of your world." And then he winked at Nick and Connor, a boyish grin spreading across his face, which the boys returned.

Eris spoke again. "You have achieved something new in the history of your species, planted the seed that will lift humanity to the next level of existence. But as Prometheus knows all too well, no great achievement comes without its price." Prometheus nodded gravely, his hand absently rubbing his side.

Vishnu spoke in a soothing tone. "We belong to this star, which you call the Sun, and its planets. But there are other beings like us who belong to other stars."

Prometheus spoke, the twinkle in his eye not dampened by the seriousness of the subject. "When you completed your battle today, when you reconciled the opposites, you initiated a new era of human history, it is true. But this integration sent a kind of shockwave through the Pleroma. It reached the nearest star, which you call Proxima Centauri, about four light years away. There are people there, not so different from you, who discovered the Gateway not long ago. But they have chosen the darker path."

"They sensed the shockwave of your battle," barked Kali fiercely, "and it caught their attention. They are warriors bent on conquest. Their planet has long ago fallen under one ruler, an absolute king who rules without mercy. And now that they know of your people's existence, they will find a way to come. And so you must prepare to fight!"

"Excuse me, oh Great Ones," said Connor hesitantly, "but what exactly is going on here? This isn't part of the Scape, is it? This is for real?"

Prometheus nodded, smiling. "This world is just as real as yours." And then he winked.

"So let me get this straight," said Izzy. "There are aliens from another star system who might attack us soon?"

"That is correct," said Eris. "You have taken the first step in the ascent to the next stage of your existence. But this ascent into a wider domain brings great danger in addition to the great gifts you will help bring to the world."

"So what you're saying," Nick mused, "is that we don't even get a minute to enjoy being the kids who took the human race to the next level before we have to start worrying about fighting off alien invaders?" Eris nodded. "Great," said Nick with a crooked grin.

"Well, I don't know about you guys," said Stefan, "but I'm ready to fight! I thought you kids were a bunch of losers—no offense—but everything is different now. You can't go through something like we went through back there and not be changed forever." He looked at Izzy with open respect and admiration. "You're a complete badass and I'd be honored to stand at your side." He stuck out his hand. After a brief hesitation, Izzy grabbed it, and they shook hands vigorously, both smiling broadly.

"I agree," said Abigail, gently taking Sophie's hand. "I still don't completely understand what just happened, but I know that I've been sad and angry for a long time, and Sophie opened up something inside of me." She looked at Sophie. "We barely know each other, and I haven't been very nice to you, but I have this crazy feeling that you're the little sister I've always wanted. I don't usually make big, emotional declarations, but I want you to know that

I trust you and I'll follow your lead." Sophie, touched, pulled Abigail in and the two girls embraced, tears streaming down their faces.

Connor looked at Nick. "Sorry about picking on you. I think I was just jealous. I didn't realize that you've been going through hard times too. You just seem like you have it all figured out, but I guess you never know what's going on with people beneath the surface, behind the mask. You're a good person. I'm going to try to be more like that." Then he grinned and said, "We don't have to hug, do we?" And all the kids laughed.

Milo spoke in a quiet voice to Ethan. "I don't totally understand what's going on either, but I think you could have destroyed me back there if you had wanted to. I think you're more powerful than you realize. Instead, you reached out and invited me in." He bowed his head for a moment, looking like he was fighting back tears, and then looked back at the younger boy. "This might all be a weird dream that I'm going to wake up from soon, and I can't believe I'm saying this, but you're the man and I'm pretty sure I'd follow you anywhere." Ethan smiled warmly and pulled Milo in for a sweetly awkward hug.

Then Vishnu's soft voice filled their heads. "It is good that you have each said these words and reconciled. You will be our emissaries, and the older ones must support and lift up the younger ones, who will be called upon to lead."

"Lead?" said Ethan. "Why us?"

"You have been chosen," said Kali. "And now you must prepare your world for the coming confrontation with the others."

"Now that you have discovered the Gateway," Prometheus said, "many more will find the Pleroma, young ones like yourselves, whose minds are not yet fixed, who remain open."

"You must show them the way," Eris said. "You must teach them what you have learned from the gifts we have given you. And in teaching, you will yourselves come to greater understanding."

"How will we know what to do?" Ethan asked.

"You will know," replied Eris. "Trust one another. Trust yourselves. We will see you soon." And with that, the light grew brighter and brighter until they had to close their eyes.

CHAPTER THIRTY-SIX
AFTER

When they opened their eyes, they were back in their seats in the auditorium. The people around them were taking off their SPECS and talking excitedly, clearly astounded by the utter reality of the experience in the Scape. The friends all sat there for a moment, looking at one another, not sure what to say. And then, as one, they all stood up and turned toward the back of the auditorium to look for the older kids. They quickly spotted them, standing in the back row, looking down at them with expressions of awe. Nick raised his hand in greeting, and Connor raised his hand in return, the others doing the same. And as they looked at each other across the packed auditorium, people putting their SPECS in their pockets and heading for the exits, they all broke out in broad smiles, and then started laughing, at first a giggle, and then hysterical fits of laughter, leaning on each other's shoulders, tears streaming down their faces.

After a minute or two, the laughter subsided and the crowd began to thin out. The four friends walked up the aisle toward the older kids who used to be their bullies, but were now their friends and allies.

"Hey, guys!" Stefan called out. "So that was pretty crazy."

"Yeah," said Izzy. "That's a word for it."

"So what now?" asked Milo, looking at Ethan.

"Well," said Ethan thoughtfully, "I guess we should all get together and figure out what to do next."

"Connor! Abigail!" The kids all turned, and there stood Jay Peterson at the door, looking none too pleased. "It's time to go."

"OK, Dad," Connor called out. And then he turned back to the others. "How about Monday after school?"

"Sounds good," said Nick. "You guys can come over to my place if you want."

"OK," said Abigail. "Let's meet by the Caves."

"You're not going to chase us this time, are you?" asked Sophie, smiling.

"Oh, God! Sorry!" said Abigail, putting her face in her hands, the other kids laughing.

"Come on!" Jay snapped. "Let's go!"

"We'll see you guys on Monday," Connor called out as he, Abigail, Stefan, and Milo walked toward the door.

The four eighth graders stood there in the mostly empty auditorium, a strange mix of euphoria and gravity filling the air around them.

"So," Nick broke the silence. "Just to reiterate, we're the chosen ones who have taken humanity to the next level, but now we have to prepare the kids of Earth to defend against alien invaders. Does that about sum it up?"

"Well," said Izzy, "when you put it like that, it does sound pretty farfetched. This is really happening, right?"

"Unless this is the most elaborate trick imaginable," Sophie said, "that's the situation. And I don't think it's a trick."

"I agree," said Ethan. "We have to prepare. The future of humanity is literally in our hands."

"Don't you mean 'figuratively'?" asked Sophie.

"Oh . . . yeah," said Ethan with a sheepish grin, and everyone laughed.

"Well, guys," said Nick, "I never thought I'd say this, but it might be time to tell the parents."

FOR FURTHER READING

The philosophical ideas touched on in *Beyond Plato's Cave* are discussed more extensively in the author's adult philosophy book *The Dynamics of Transformation: Tracing an Emerging World View.*

You can learn more about *The Philosophy Club* series at PhilosophyClub.info, and be sure to keep an eye out for Book Two!

ACKNOWLEDGMENTS

Thanks to my friends for inspiring parts of this book, in roughly chronological order: Brian Pacula, Greg Patterson, Andreas Stringer, Bayard Culley, David Hughes, Jared Rock, Elina North, Shannon Mulholland, Will Bledsoe, Robert Garrison, JR Minkel, William Tyler, Brandon Wiley, Rebecca Kruger, Jessica Belasco, Sarah Rennick, John Meitzen, Jeremy Liebman, Brent Pennington, Andy McCallister, Arun Nair, Kirk Shinkle, James Case-Leal, Gabriel Blair, Gregory DeGroat, Justin Dake, Stephanie von Behr, Matthew Stoulil, Kevin Drost, Christian Ebert, Will Grissom, Rachael Andersen-Watts, Eli Bortz . . .

And thanks to my mother, Carol Orsborn, for passing on the love of writing and teaching me to go deep; to my father, Dan Orsborn, for passing on the love of music and always supporting my creativity; to my sister, Jody Orsborn, for being my fellow music aficionado; to my father-in-law, Don Edwards, for being The Donski; to my mother-in-law, Susan

Edwards, for being my aesthetic guru; to my eight-year-old son, Mason Maxwell, for listening avidly while I read him the entire *Harry Potter* series even though he could have read it himself (we're reading *The Hobbit* now), for reminding me how to think like a kid, and for being a generally awesome guy; to my two-year-old son, Dylan Maxwell, for being a cute, hilarious little guy; and last, but very, very much not least, to my wife, Ginny Maxwell, for talking through this book with me every step of the way, helping develop the characters, come up with the plot, and work out all the details. We basically created this story together, and I just wrote it down.

ABOUT THE AUTHOR

In addition to *The Philosophy Club* series, Grant Maxwell is the author of *The Dynamics of Transformation: Tracing an Emerging World View*, *How Does It Feel?: Elvis Presley, The Beatles, Bob Dylan, and the Philosophy of Rock and Roll*, and *The Walk*, an illustrated children's book. He is an editor at Persistent Press and *Archai: The Journal of Archetypal Cosmology*, and he has served as an editor at Vanderbilt University Press and as a professor of English at Baruch College and Lehman College in New York. He has written for the American Philosophical Association blog, *American Songwriter* magazine, the *Journal of Religion and Popular Culture*, and the *Archai* journal, and he holds a PhD from the City University of New York's Graduate Center. He's also a musician, and he lives in Nashville, Tennessee with his wife and two sons.

Made in the USA
Middletown, DE
02 October 2018